*The Golem and the Wondrous
Deeds of the Maharal of Prague*

Other Books by Curt Leviant

Novels

The Yemenite Girl
Passion in the Desert
The Man Who Thought He Was Messiah
Partita in Venice
Diary of an Adulterous Woman
*Ladies and Gentlemen, the Original Music of the Hebrew Alphabet and
     Weekend in Mustara* (two novellas)
A Novel of Klass
Kafka's Son (in French, 2009)

Translations from Yiddish

Stories and Satires, by Sholom Aleichem
Old Country Tales, by Sholom Aleichem
Some Laughter, Some Tears, by Sholom Aleichem
From the Fair, the Autobiography of Sholom Aleichem
The Song of Songs, by Sholom Aleichem
The Agunah, by Chaim Grade
The Yeshiva, by Chaim Grade
The Yeshiva, vol. II, *Masters and Disciples,* by Chaim Grade
The Seven Little Lanes, by Chaim Grade
The Jewish Government and Other Stories, by Lamed Shapiro
The Heart-Stirring Sermon and Other Stories, by Avraham Reisen
More Stories From My Father's Court, by Isaac Bashevis Singer
The Jewish Book of Fables, by Eliezer Shtaynbarg

Edited Texts from the Hebrew with Introductions

King Artus: A Hebrew Arthurian Romance of 1279
Masterpieces of Hebrew Literature: A Treasury of 2000 Years of Jewish Creativity

The Golem

and the Wondrous Deeds
of the Maharal of Prague

Yudl Rosenberg

Translated from the Hebrew and
Edited and with an Introduction and Notes by

Curt Leviant

Yale University Press   New Haven and London

This work was supported by a grant from the National Endowment for the Humanities, whose assistance is gratefully acknowledged.

Published with assistance from the Mary Cady Tew Memorial Fund.

page 1: Hebrew title page of the first edition of Yudl Rosenberg's *Niflo'es Maharal* (The Golem and the Wondrous Deeds of the Maharal). Published in Piotrkow, Poland, 1909.

Designed by Sonia L. Shannon.
Set in Bulmer type by Integrated Publishing Solutions.

Printed in the United States of America.

The Library of Congress has cataloged the hardcover edition as follows:
Rozenberg, Yehudah Yudl, 1865–1935.
    [Nifla'ot Maharal. English.]
    The golem and the wondrous deeds of the Maharal of Prague / Yudl Rosenberg ; translated from the Hebrew and edited and with an introduction and notes by Curt Leviant.
    p.   cm.
    Includes bibliographical references.
    ISBN: 978-0-300-12204-6 (cloth : alk. paper)
    1. Golem.   2. Judah Loew ben Bezalel, ca. 1525–1609—Legends.
    3. Blood accusation—Legends.   4. Legends, Jewish.
    I. Leviant, Curt.   II. Title.
    BM531.R6913 2007
    398.2′089924—dc22   2006032509

ISBN: 978-0-300-14320-1 (pbk. : alk. paper)

A catalogue record for this book is available from the British Library.

This paper meets the requirements of ANSI/NISO Z39.48-1992 (Permanence of Paper).

It contains 30 percent postconsumer waste (PCW) and is certified by the Forest Stewardship Council (FSC).

10 9 8 7 6 5 4 3 2 1

For
Elie Wiesel
and
Sol Gittleman
with affection and esteem

CONTENTS

ACKNOWLEDGMENTS

Thanks to Gilad Gevaryahu, Professor Ira Robinson, and Professor Moshe Pelli for providing pertinent articles; to Aaron Brody, Yudl Rosenberg's great-great-grandson, for photocopies of Rosenberg's bilingual edition of *Niflo'es Maharal* and other books by Rosenberg; and to Rabbi Avi Kelman, Dr. Daniel Matt, and Professor Moshe Idel for help with kabbala terminology.

My gratitude too to Carla Hanauer of the Yeshiva University Gottesman Library for generous assistance and copies of needed articles.

And a special thanks to Professor Lewis Glinert, whose article on the golem sparked my interest in this subject.

The word *golem* is an ancient one, probably more than three thousand years old. It makes its first—and only—appearance in the Bible, in a slightly different form in Psalm 139, verse 16: "Your eyes have seen my unformed limbs [or embryo, *golmi*]." Hundreds of years later the word as we know it, *golem,* is used in the Talmud, where it means "unshaped matter" or "unfinished creation," and, in one case, in Ethics of the Fathers 5:9, the opposite of a wise man—a boor, a simpleton, which anticipates the much later evocative Yiddish expression "leymener geylem" (literally, a clay golem) to signify a fool. But not until the Middle Ages did "golem" assume its current meaning, "artificial man," or "creature of clay."

In Jewish culture and the Hebrew literary tradition, the concept of a golem goes back about sixteen centuries to a Talmudic sage from Babylonia named Rava, who reputedly created a man, but one who could not talk. Although this creature was not called a golem, the legend surrounding

Rava's creation can be viewed as an antecedent for subsequent golem tales. In the Talmud, Tractate Sanhedrin 65b, we read: "Rava b'ra gavra" רבא ברא גברא—Rava created a man. In its very construction and anagramic quality, the three-word sentence radiates a mysticism of its own, for the letters "b/v" ב, "r" ר, and "a" א appear in all three words. Rashi, the classic eleventh-century French exegete to the Bible and Talmud, comments: "This creature was created with the help of *Sefer Yetzira* [*Book of Creation,* a seminal kabbalistic text of the third to sixth centuries C.E.], for they learned the proper combinations of letters of God's name."

The Talmud goes on to relate that after Rava created this man, he sent him to Rav Zeira, who spoke to this creation but it did not answer him. Why? Because artificially created men do not have the ability to speak—and Rava's anthropoid followed the rules. Rav Zeira then told him: "You have been created by one of my colleagues . . . Return to dust." Over the centuries, from the Middle Ages to modern times, and in many lands, these famous lines in Sanhedrin, by now a kind of ur-text, have achieved an iconic status. This passage—a centerpiece in all excurses on the golem—was analyzed and commented upon by many mystics. Leading figures in world Jewry, kabbalists, scholars, and rabbis, Nachmanides among them, were magnetized by these few but potent words that were examined from the perspective of magic, religion, spirituality, theosophy, and intellect.

In golem legends there are various ways of bringing the clay creature to life. One is the method Rashi cited—reciting the proper combinations of letters of God's name. Another is inserting God's name into the golem's mouth or affixing it to his forehead. In our text, Yudl Rosenberg's *The Golem and the Wondrous Deeds of the Maharal of Prague,* the golem is vivified by three rabbis marching around him seven times while saying various names of God in special kabbalistic permutations. Yet another dramatic method of giving life is to insert into the golem the three letter word "emet" אמת, truth, in Jewish mysticism one of the less well-known names of God. And when the time comes to take away his spirit, the first letter, aleph א, which stands for "Elohim" or God, is removed, leaving only the two letters that form the word "met" מת, death. Whatever the recipe, God's name is a necessary ingredient. Without it, no life would be infused into the golem.

The golem has been a continuous presence in Jewish lore since the Middle Ages. The great eleventh-century Spanish Hebrew poet, Shlomo ibn Gabirol, is said to have made a female golem out of wood to serve as a housemaid. By the fifteenth century, stories of the golem were spreading throughout German Jewry, and by the seventeenth century, golem tales had become common in the oral traditions of European Jews.

The most vivid, pervasive and influential version of the golem legend emerges from sixteenth-century Prague and is indelibly linked with Rabbi Loew (1525–1609), the famous spiritual leader of the Prague Jewish community, known as the Maharal (an acronym for **M**orenu **Ha-Ra**v **L**oew). The legend of the Maharal and the golem he made for his own personal use, to fetch water and chop wood, makes its debut in the first third of the nineteenth century. None of the Maharal's works nor those of his contemporaries mentions the golem legend, nor do any writings of the Maharal's disciples. Furthermore, whatever tales of the golem circulated either orally or in writing had him doing domestic tasks and nothing more.

But then, in 1909, in Warsaw, a singular event occurred that changed the direction of the legend for the rest of the twentieth century and prompted the efflorescence of this story in so many branches of art. It was the appearance of *Niflo'es Maharal* (actual full title, The Wondrous Deeds of the Maharal of Prague with the Golem), by Yudl

Rosenberg—a short book of stories about the Prague rabbi and the golem he created.

As an Orthodox rabbi in Warsaw, in a community that viewed fiction as frivolous and utterly outside the Jewish tradition of Torah study, Rosenberg had to disguise his authorship of the book. He resorted to the classic ruse of the "discovered" manuscript, à la Defoe in *Robinson Crusoe* and Swift in *Gulliver's Travels,* who also pretended their books were written by someone else, as did Alexander Dumas, who in his preface to his *Three Musketeers* (1844) claims he discovered his text in the Royal Library. To an unsuspecting public, Rosenberg was able to pass off his own book as if it had been written hundreds of years earlier by the Maharal's son-in-law, Rabbi Isaac Katz. (To this day some people still believe this.) Rosenberg's claim that the Maharal's son-in-law wrote the book naturally enhanced its value. Readers were more eager to buy a book about the Maharal and the golem written by a relative than one by an unknown Warsaw rabbi. Here is pseudepigraphic literature at its best, reflecting the same attitude of classical works like the author of the anonymous second-century B.C.E. *Testament of the Twelve Sons* who claimed that each of Jacob's sons wrote his particular testament.

In his publisher's preface, Rosenberg contends he bought a copy of the manuscript that had remained undiscovered in the great library of Metz (elsewhere he calls it the Royal Library), in northern France, for three hundred years, and will now share this story with the reading public. In reality, no such library existed and, needless to say, no one has ever seen this three-hundred-year-old manuscript. There is no doubt that Yudl Rosenberg concocted this fiction within a fiction, just as he changed the golem from a servant of one man, the Maharal, into a servant of the entire Jewish community.

Yehuda Yudl Rosenberg was born in Russian Poland in 1859 (the same year as Sholom Aleichem). He received a traditional yeshiva education and was hailed as a young genius. After serving as rabbi in several Polish towns he ended his European rabbinic career in Warsaw. To enhance his meager income he wrote books on halakha (Jewish law) and midrash, translated sections of the classic kabbala text, *The Zohar,* from Aramaic to Hebrew, and created works of fiction (always disguising his own authorship in this genre), including an anthology of stories he edited about Elijah the Prophet that included some tales of his own composition.

Rosenberg emigrated to Canada in 1913, when he was

in his mid-fifties, and held rabbinic posts first in Toronto and then in Montreal, where he died in 1935, honored and esteemed in North America and Europe—but still unrecognized for his vast literary output. Despite his twenty-seven books, almost all in Hebrew, he never gained fame as a Hebrew writer. Although Rosenberg is briefly mentioned in an *Encyclopedia Judaica* article on "golem," he has no entry under his own name.

Unique among his Orthodox peers, Yudl Rosenberg read widely in secular literature, displaying an interest in modern Hebrew writing and books on science in Hebrew. After mastering Russian he was able to read works from other languages in Russian translation. Despite his being labeled a folk writer, Rosenberg was not a naïf. He was familiar with the sorcerer's apprentice motif, which he incorporated into one of his stories where the golem, told to fill the water barrel, keeps on pouring until the room is flooded. Rosenberg also read a Russian version of Arthur Conan Doyle's Sherlock Holmes story "The Jew's Breastplate," which he adapted for another book, *Khoshen Mishpat* (The Breastplate of Judgment). That Rosenberg learned well the technique of composing a detective story can be seen in some of the tales in *Niflo'es Maharal.*

Rosenberg's business acumen, as well as his need to sell books, is evident at the end of *Niflo'es Maharal,* where he has a one-and-a-half page chapter entitled "Advertisement" (not included in this English version). Here he lists seven of his books, ranging in price from five kopecks to thirty kopecks, including *Niflo'es Maharal,* available from the publisher at forty kopecks. Rosenberg notes that both the Hebrew and the Yiddish versions can also be bought at a local bookseller, Aharon Tzeylengold, whose Warsaw address is listed on the title page of the work as well. On a final page the author repeats, in one paragraph, the offer he has made in Chapter 2, of the availability—through him—of another Maharal manuscript for 800 kroner. This seems to be another of the author's clever devices to support the authenticity of the *Niflo'es Maharal* manuscript. And the steep price—800 kroner (the equivalent of $800 vis-à-vis the 5–40 cent price for his books)— virtually ensured that no one would inquire about this undoubtedly invented manuscript.

Rosenberg's Hebrew narrative of the enduring golem legend took the European Jewish community by storm in 1909, a fact that is often noted in writings about the author. At the same time he created a Yiddish version. "We have translated this book into Yiddish," Rosenberg writes on the title page, "to enable people of all classes to enjoy this illuminating work." The popularity of both versions prompted a pirated bilingual edition in 1913 (evidently hastily and carelessly compiled, for it is full of errors), with a slight change of title. Rosenberg's name was omitted, but, curiously, Reb Aharon Tzeylengold is listed on the title page as the bookseller of this unauthorized bilingual book, just as he was listed on the title pages of the Hebrew original and the Yiddish translation.

Rosenberg's prose style is a rabbinic Hebrew into which lines from the Bible, the Talmud, the liturgy, and occasionally, phrases from the Kabbala, blend seamlessly. Rather than sounding recondite, these more than 150 quotations from all layers of Hebrew would be well known to any reader who had a traditional Jewish education and who observed Jewish customs. For instance, to depict the salvation of the Jews from annihilation, as seen in the Book of Esther, the writer skillfully draws on these familiar and oft-quoted phrases and verses.

Eli Yassif, an Israeli scholar who has written about Rosenberg, noted that his "Hebrew and Yiddish versions are identical." But Yassif evidently only glanced at Rosenberg's Yiddish text, for a closer comparison reveals that in almost every chapter of *Niflo'es Maharal* lines from the original Hebrew are missing in the Yiddish; one chapter is altogether left out; large portions of the Christian-Jewish theological debate are omitted; nuanced Hebrew textual details disappear; and actions of the protagonists are at times altered. Also left out of the Yiddish version are passages that contain kabbalistic material. And the Yiddish lacks the finely textured Hebrew with its plethora of Biblical quotations, Talmudic phrases, and lines from liturgical texts.

Niflo'es Maharal was read all over Europe, going through a number of editions. In 1917, a German version by Chayim Bloch appeared in Vienna; this too was a pirated edition. It is ironic that Rosenberg passed off his original work as written by the Maharal's son-in-law, while Bloch, the translator/adapter of *Niflo'es Maharal,* blatantly arrogated Rosenberg's book as if it were his own creation. Bloch then visited the United States, basked in the glory of his book, elicited sympathy for his impoverished state, and tried to collect money to subsidize his other books—without ever even giving a shred of credit to the real author.

Rosenberg's stories even reached as far as the Middle East via a Judeo-Persian translation and to North Africa in Judeo-Arabic. The book also achieved the status of a folk tale, versions of which were narrated orally in different places.

Rosenberg's rendition now shaped—and indelibly reshaped—
the basic format of the golem legend.

*The Golem and the Wondrous Deeds of the Maharal of
Prague* contains some twenty stories, many interlocking; one
could almost call it a novel because it follows a group of characters: the omnipresent Maharal; his trusted assistant, always
referred to as "the old shamesh, Reb Avrohom Chaim"; the
Maharal's archenemy, the viciously anti-Semitic priest Thaddeus; the goodly cardinal, Jan Salvester; the beneficent King
Rudolf; and, of course, the faithful and always dependable
golem who is given the endearing Yiddish name, Yossele, an
intimate diminutive of Yosef (Joseph).

By having a name—the first time a golem is named, thus
humanizing him even more—Yossele the golem rises up over
the previous nameless golems who were merely the result of
some successful magical or mystical technique. There was
nothing personal, or personable, about them. But in Rosenberg's book Yossele truly becomes human. After he is attacked
and injured, he is bandaged and tended and rests three days
in bed. Later, he signals his desire to take revenge on his attackers. Although Yossele cannot speak, he can read and
write. He follows complicated instructions meticulously and
successfully and initiates certain actions on his own.

Because Yossele has these human qualities—another of Rosenberg's brilliant innovations, which will be followed in subsequent golem novels stories and plays written by other writers in various languages—Yossele's behavior distances him from a purely dumb artificial humanoid. It is noteworthy too that, unlike previous golems in legend, including the one that he served the Maharal, Rosenberg's Yossele does not run amok; the gentle golem does not have to be destroyed because he is violent; he was created for a purpose and that purpose has been fulfilled.

For all of these reasons, and for his faithfulness and near humanity, we feel a real sense of loss when the time comes for the Maharal to undo the golem's vitality and return him to dust. The reader cannot help but bid a sad goodbye to the good golem.

To the major and ever-alluring theme of golem-making, Rosenberg added the Jewish element of salvation and protection. He has Rabbi Loew, the Maharal, create a golem not to help with domestic chores but to fight the false accusation of ritual murder leveled against the Jews—the infamous blood libel, the thousand-year-old European Christian canard that Jews need the blood of a Christian child to bake matzas for

Passover. By adding the theme of the golem as rescuer, Rosenberg fused the anti-Semitism that pervaded Europe during his own time with that of the golem—not unlike Superman, the comic strip hero created in the late 1930s by two American Jews to protect the innocent and battle evil.

The myth of the golem who defends Jews during times of persecution, which many people nowadays mistakenly trace back to the sixteenth century, is actually a modern literary invention, a brilliant stroke created single-handedly by Yudl Rosenberg. Henceforth, this innovation becomes a standard aspect in all retellings of the Maharal-golem legend. No wonder Yosef Dan, a folklore expert at the Hebrew University, called Rosenberg's golem story Hebrew literature's most important contribution to world literature in the twentieth century.

Rosenberg's plot has all the ingredients to appeal to a wide range of readers: fantasy, romance, kabbala and mysticism, adventure, suspense, detective story motifs, humor, false accusations, riveting courtroom trials, a duel of wills between leaders of the Jewish and Christian communities, a kindly and wise hero pitted against his hateful antagonist, and the mute and powerful golem whom the Maharal's magical amulet occasionally makes invisible.

Besides bringing religio-cultural authenticity and relevance to his book, Rosenberg also told a superb story and knew how to use comedic relief and bring legendary and historic personalities to life. Because he was an expert in kabbala, he was able to include in his descriptions of the golem-making all the magical atmosphere inherent in the *Book of Creation.* It is not surprising, then, that Rosenberg's novel about the golem—itself a creature stemming from the kabbalistic tradition—is so full of kabbalistic links. From the man who "possesses the sparks of . . ." to the ceremony of creating the golem; from the Hebrew alphabet possessing a special power to the idea of combining letters into words that form the Divine Name; from seeing Hebrew letters in colors to the golem's gift of distinguishing one hour from the next because of different scents that emanate from the lower Garden of Eden—Rosenberg's book is replete with the spirit of kabbala which allows for such unreal or even surreal events in the story like an amulet for invisibility, letters changing colors in the Siddur, questions asked and divinely answered in dreams, and other supernatural events that compete favorably with mid-twentieth-century literature's magic realism.

In his depiction of characters, Rosenberg is always fair. Of course, the Maharal is wise and omnipotent, able to penetrate all mysteries. But the golem is no Superman; once some Jewish toughs ambush him and cast him into a well, where he is injured and nearly drowns. The priest Thaddeus is the novel's Haman, a source of unmitigated evil. But King Rudolf is fair, even supportive. There is no whiff of state-sponsored anti-Semitism, like in Czarist Russia; nor is there widespread popular hatred of Jews like in Austria, Germany, and Poland before and during World War II. Anti-Semites exist; they surface during a blood libel trial, but when they intend violence the efficient police restrain them, and ultimately justice prevails. Balancing the evil priest is a decent cardinal. After the even-handed theological debate between the Maharal and the priests, the cardinal praises the Maharal; and later, when Thaddeus initiates a blood libel and the cardinal, knowing that this is a false accusation, must reluctantly submit a protocol to the court, he also quietly sends a copy to the Maharal to enable him to make adequate preparations to defend his community.

In Rosenberg's book the criminal justice system is also fair. Although Jews accused of blood libel are brought to court, the judges are open to evidence showing that the accusation is false, whereupon the evil conspirators who have committed perjury are punished. The police in Prague are more like a Western force; they are not a brutal arm of a repressive regime.

Jews accused of ritual murder are indeed arrested—but freed when the falseness of the accusation is revealed. Likewise, when the police catch a Christian about to cast a dead Christian child into a Jew's home before Passover, they arrest him and bring him to judgment.

Rosenberg's characters are not stereotypes: a Jewish tannery owner is not totally compassionate in his treatment of an injured young Christian worker. In revenge, his two older brothers also employed in the tannery, plot a blood libel against their boss. But these two nasty brothers, who almost succeed in their fabricated accusation, are not wholly evil either: they care for their poor, elderly mother and tend to and protect their younger brother.

Rosenberg's *Golem* has an impressive number of innovations, all of which are used in subsequent retellings of the golem legend in various art forms. The author is the first to:

1.   name the golem;
2.   humanize him: he can get hurt, recover, request permission for revenge against his attackers;
3.   assign the golem tasks other than domestic chores;
4.   give the golem the ability to read and write;

5. have him follow complicated orders;
6. let the golem initiate actions;
7. have the golem fight for and protect the Jewish people against the blood libel and other injustices;
8. let the golem expire peacefully and not as a consequence of his unrestrained fury; and
9. make the golem a thoroughly beneficent creature.

The chief ingredient for the success of *The Golem and the Wondrous Deeds of the Maharal of Prague,* it can be argued, was—given the difficult circumstances European Jews faced at the beginning of the twentieth century—the book's portrayal of the victory of the Jews and the triumph of good over evil. Ten years before the 1909 publication of Rosenberg's book, the European Jewish community had been shaken by an infamous blood libel case near Prague (despite Rosenberg's story, there were no blood libels in Prague during the Maharal's tenure as chief rabbi in the late sixteenth century). The notorious pogroms in Kishinev, Russia, in 1903 and in 1905—the bloodiest outbreak of government organized anti-Semitic violence in years—were the culmination of waves of anti-Jewish excesses in Russia at the end of the nineteenth century that forced hundreds of thousands of Jews to flee to the freedom and safety of America. A book like Rosenberg's, then, where the Jews overcome their tormentors, was just the escapist reading the Jews needed and wanted.

What is most fascinating about this groundbreaking collection of stories is that in the decades after its publication, besides several translations, a spurt of artistic creation utilizes the golem theme: Gustav Meyrink's kabbalistically inspired novel, *The Golem* (1915), in German; H. Leivick's Yiddish verse drama, *The Golem* (1921), where the evil priest, Thaddeus, reappears attempting a blood libel similar in plot and setting to Chapter 15 in Rosenberg's book; the classic silent expressionist German film *Der Golem*, directed by and starring Paul Wegener (1921); the French film *Le Golem*, directed by Julien Duvivier (1936). Many operas and ballets were written on this same theme in the succeeding decades to the end of the twentieth and the beginning of the twenty-first century, including a production by the Prague State Opera in 2001. Jorge Luis Borges dealt with the golem theme in "El Golem" (1958), a poem that inspired an elaborate golem festival in Prague in October 2002 that included films, readings, song recitals, and chamber music concerts.

Following are two examples of how Rosenberg's innovative twist to the role of the golem influenced subsequent works.

The passage below, which shows the Maharal in action without the golem, is from a collection of Jewish tales and legends that are included in a book *Sippurim,* by L. Weisel, published in Prague in 1847. Weisel states that he transcribed legends that had been passed down orally from generation to generation. In the story below the Maharal, aided by his study of kabbalistic texts, especially *Sefer Yetzira,* the *Book of Creation,* is known to have magical powers.

The Emperor once had a strange whim; he wanted to see the Patriarchs and the sons of Jacob and ordered Rabbi Loew to summon them from their graves. The Rabbi consented, but made the condition that the Emperor must not laugh no matter what he saw. The day and place were fixed and the summoning began in a secluded room in the castle. The Patriarchs and the founders of the tribes appeared one after the other in their true form, and the Emperor was astounded at the size and power of these men of the days long gone by; for each of them showed himself with all his attributes. But when the fleet Naftali skimmed over the ears of corn and stalks of flax, the Emperor could not contain himself and began to laugh. At once the apparitions disappeared and the ceiling of the room began to descend. It would have crushed the Emperor, had not Rabbi Loew arrested it with the help of the Kabbala. It is said that the fallen ceiling can still be seen today in the room, which is kept closed. At least so the story goes among the Jewish people.

In the silent film, *The Golem*, Wegener used this scene—with a slight but important variation—as a crucial segment in his story. It is a perfect example of the influence that Rosenberg's book had on Wegener's retelling of the legend.

In the film, the Emperor has issued an edict of expulsion against Jews. The Maharal requests an audience with the Emperor, who grants it because of the rabbi's past service to the ruler. The Maharal brings the golem with him. In a film within a film, the Maharal magically shows the Emperor and his court the Patriarchs and the Exodus from Egypt. He has previously warned everyone not to laugh, but the courtiers do not heed him. As the laughter swells the vault of the ceiling begins to crumble and descend. The frightened Emperor tells the Maharal that if he saves him, he will rescind the expulsion edict. The golem lifts his hands and supports the falling ceiling, saving everyone. True to the character that Rosenberg invented, here too the golem saves the Jewish people.

In one of the stories of *Niflo'es Maharal* a trial takes place in the synagogue and the soul of a dead midwife who has exchanged two babies at birth has to testify. The Maharal gives his staff to his shamesh and tells him to bring back the woman's soul from the cemetery, whereupon she has to stand behind a partition. The congregants tremble with fear but the Maharal calms them. S. Anski's famous Yiddish play, *The Dybbuk* (1920), and its 1937 film version have a marvelous scene near the end where a trial takes place. One of the participants is a dead man. The rabbi gives his shamesh his staff and tells him to go to the cemetery to bring back the soul of the dead man to the synagogue where the trial is taking place. The dead man is to stand behind the partition. Meanwhile, the congregants tremble with fear. Given the similarity of so many points, Anski doubtless read Rosenberg's popular book and adapted that scene for his *Dybbuk*.

In contemporary belles letters, two Nobel laureates have contributed to the extension of the Maharal/golem legend: Isaac Bashevis Singer in *The Golem* (1982) and Elie Wiesel in his version, *The Golem* (1983). Both these works were published as children's books, but not necessarily directed solely at youngsters, for the exciting and tension-filled narratives can also be read by adults as morality plays. And Michael Chabon used the golem theme in his Pulitzer Prize–winning novel *The Amazing Adventures of Kavalier and Clay* (2001).

Some have even contended that robots, computers, and artificial intelligence are outgrowths of the golem legend. Perhaps it is no accident that Prague, so imbued with golem stories, was the place where the Czech playwright Karel Capek wrote his famous drama about robots, *R. U. R.* (1921), which introduced the word "robot."

Making something inanimate come to life—whether it is Pygmalion's statue in the ancient world, the attempts of the alchemist Paracelsus in the Middle Ages, the hero of Mary Shelley's *Frankenstein* (1818) or Carlo Collodi's *Pinocchio* (1883)—has always been an electrifying folk and literary motif. Given the abiding interest in the twentieth century in this intriguing theme, and keeping in mind that since ancient times, both in the Jewish and non-Jewish world, man has had an incessant enchantment with creating a living creature (after all, *imitatio dei* is a powerful impulse), it is amazing that Yudl Rosenberg's influential work had never been translated from his original Hebrew into English, a literary lacuna that has now been filled.

Curt Leviant

זה ספר

נפלאות מהר"ל

בו יסופר האותות והמופתים והנפלאות מאת מרן ורבן של כל בני
הגולה הצדיק והקדוש גאון הגאונים נזר ישראל ועטרת ישועתו
ומלאה הארץ צדקתו וגדולתו הנקרא

מהר"ל מפראג זצוקלה"ה

אשר הפליא לעשות גדולות ונוראות על ידי

הגולם

אשר ברא בכח חכמת הקבלה להלחם נגד עלילת דם , אשר נפרצה
בימיו ולברר האמת לעין כל כי נקיים ישראל מקלון הזה :

הספר הזה נכתב ע"י הגאון הגדול כו' וכו' מוהר"י כ"ץ זצ"ל , חתנא
דבי נשיאה של המהר"ל . והיה ספון בהביבליאטיקה הגדולה דעיר מיץ ,
ואחרי חורבנה עוד לפני מאה שנה שנשדרה במלחמה , נפלו הרבה
ספרים עתיקים וכתבי יד בידי עשירי העיר . והרבה יגעתי ועמלתי עד
שמצאה ידי להשיג העתקה הזאת , כאשר יראה הקורא בהקדמה :

יצא לאור ע"י הרב וכו' ר' יודל ראזענבערג רומ"ץ בעיר ווארשא .

בהוצאות המו"ס ר' אה,ן ציילינגאלד בווארשא נאלעווקי 32

פיעטרקוב

בדפוס החדש המשובח של ר' חנוך העניך פאלמאן נ"י

שנת   תרס"ט   לפ"ק

СФЕРЪ НИФЛУОСЪ МАГАРАЛЪ
т. е. гисторія Раввина „Магарала"

Тип. Эноха Фольмана г. Петроковъ 1909 г.

1

Publisher's Preface

DEAR READERS! I AM HEREWITH presenting you with a delightful and precious treasure that until now had lain hidden for some three hundred years in the great library of Metz. That the Maharal had miraculously created a living golem from loam and clay was an oral tradition well known to everyone. However, over a period of time, people began expressing doubts to the point where enlightened men were already denying this entire incident and dismissing it as nothing but a folk legend.

But the fact is that when the great gaon, our saintly master, Rabbi Yechezkel Landau, of blessed memory, the author of *Known in Judah,* was the Rabbi of Prague, he established the truth of this story: that in the attic of the Great Synagogue lay the golem whom the Maharal had created. It is widely known that one day Rabbi Landau fasted and went to the

ritual bath. After commanding ten of his students to recite
Psalms on his behalf, he wrapped himself in his tallis and
tefillin and ascended alone to the attic. The gaon spent a long
while up there. When he descended, his face was marked by
terror and dread. He proclaimed that henceforth he was making even more stringent the Maharal's prohibition that no one
ever dare go up to the attic.

However, after several decades many people once again
began to doubt the truth of the story because this incident
was not recorded in any book of Jewish history. But eventually the truth surfaces. And now all Jews will know and realize that this entire matter was written down by the Maharal's
son-in-law, the great gaon, our saintly master, Rabbi Yitzchok
Katz, of blessed memory, as can be seen by some stories
herein and by the Maharal's remarks printed at the end of
the book.

But all this has long been stored in the great library of
Metz along with many other of the Maharal's books in manuscript, and I thank God for helping me to acquire this copy
from my kinsman, Rabbi Chaim Scharfstein of Metz. I have
spent a lot of money on this and, besides the cost, I have
worked hard to prepare this book for publication. And so I

hope that every seeker of knowledge will be grateful to me for this labor. Whoever sees this book will surely not be able to put it down and will find a place for it in his library.

The publisher,
The insignificant Yudl Rosenberg of Warsaw

2

Bill of Sale

I HEREWITH INFORM THE GENERAL public that it is forbidden to reprint this book without my permission, for I purchased it at full value and I own it in perpetuity. Therefore, I am displaying the bill of sale for this book for everyone to see:

Praised be God

My signature below is testimony, as efficacious as one hundred valid witnesses, that I, the undersigned, Chaim Scharfstein of the holy community of Metz, have sold to my kinsman, the illustrious rabbi and scholar, our master Rabbi Yehuda Yudl Rosenberg, rabbinic judge and spiritual leader of the holy community of Warsaw, the book that was copied from the holy manuscript of the renowned gaon, our master, the saintly Rabbi Yitzchok Katz, of blessed memory, son-in-law of the saintly Maharal, of blessed memory, who indited in his holy manuscript some of the great wondrous deeds, marvels and miracles that his father-in-law accomplished in the city of Prague, when he created the golem and used him to save the Jews from various misfortunes, especially the calamity of the blood libel.

This book was located here in the great library of the holy community of Metz. I sold a copy of this book at full value to my kinsman, the aforementioned illustrious rabbi of the city of Warsaw, to be his possession, and his alone, in perpetuity.

From this moment on I am placing an absolute injunction upon myself never again to sell to anyone else another copy of the above manuscript.

At the same time I announce to the public that I am in possession of another long manuscript by the holy Maharal about the supreme sanctity of the Sabbath, entitled *The Greatness of Israel,* which comprises more than one hundred octavo pages. I will sell this manuscript to the first person who offers 800 crowns. Any interested buyer is directed to my kinsman, the above-mentioned gaon and rabbi from the city of Warsaw.

The first of Adar, 5669 [1909] here in the holy city of Metz
Chaim Scharfstein

3

*The History of the Great Gaon, the Holy,
Supernal Maharal of Prague, May the Memory
of that Righteous, Saintly Man Be a Blessing
for Life in the World to Come*

THE HOLY MAHARAL WAS BORN in Worms in the year
5273 (1513) during the first Seder of Passover. His saintly father, Bezalel, of blessed memory, was an extremely righteous
man. With his very birth the Maharal brought salvation and
deliverance to the world. The Jews were then suffering from
unrelenting persecution by the Christian nations, who
claimed that the Jews needed Christian blood for their
Passover matzas. Hardly a Passover festival occurred in the
lands of Bohemia, Moravia, Hungary, and Spain without a
dead Christian boy being thrown into a hidden corner of a

rich Jew's property in order to accuse him of murdering the child and using his blood for ritual purposes.

In Worms too, that Passover, people secretly plotted a blood libel against the Maharal's father, the above-mentioned Rabbi Bezalel.

Here is what happened:

A Christian carrying a dead child in a sack, stole into the Jewish quarter intent upon casting the corpse through a small window into the cellar of Rabbi Bezalel's house. Rabbi Bezalel's wife was pregnant then, in her seventh month, but during the Seder of the first night of Passover she suddenly felt birth pangs. A big tumult ensued in the house and amid cries and shouts some men ran outside to summon a midwife.

At that moment, the Christian carrying the dead child in a sack was not far from the house. Seeing men running toward him in a panic and loudly shouting, the Christian thought they had discovered his plot and were hastening to seize him. So he turned and fled to the Christian neighborhood.

He was so frightened and confused he kept running at breakneck speed even after he had reached the Christian part of town because he thought the Jews were still after him to seize him.

But the police and night watchmen, noticing a man running helter-skelter and carrying something in a sack on this shoulders, and seeing far off the men from Rabbi Bezalel's house also rushing in the same direction, assumed he was a thief fleeing with stolen goods and that the others were in pursuit to retrieve the theft.

The policemen caught and searched him. When they saw what he had, they brought him to the chief of police, where he was vigorously interrogated. Only then did the man confess that he had brought the dead boy there in order to accuse Rabbi Bezalel of the blood libel. The police arrested and brought the man to judgment.

News of this salvation immediately spread through the entire city. Rabbi Bezalel prophesied regarding the newborn boy, saying: "This one will comfort us and save us from the blood libel." He named the boy Yehuda Leib, after the verse: "Judah is a lion's whelp; on prey, my son, have you grown."

4

The Maharal's Battle Against the Blood Libel

IN THE YEAR 1572, THE MAHARAL was invited from
Posen, where he had been the rabbi, to become Chief Rabbi
and head of the rabbinical court of the holy community of
Prague. He had already achieved world fame on account of
his great wisdom in all branches of knowledge and in all the
languages. And because of this he was beloved and admired
by the learned gentiles.

The Biblical verse "A man who excels at his work shall
attend upon kings" described him, for he was also esteemed
and respected by King Rudolf. Therefore, it was within his
power to battle against the enemies of Israel who mocked and
insulted us because of the blood libel until he attained the
upper hand and triumphed over them.

King Rudolf promised the Maharal he would not permit
any court in his land to level the accusation of ritual murder

against the Jews. When the Maharal was appointed rabbi of the holy community of Prague, it was a calamitous time for the Jews and they suffered greatly from the blood libel. On account of that despicable accusation, the blood of many Jewish souls innocent of any blame was gratuitously spilled like water. Thereupon, the Maharal gave an order to spread the word openly to all the nations that he was prepared to stand straight like a wall to battle against the blood libel with all his might and to exculpate his fellow Jews from this despicable false accusation.

5

The Maharal's Suggestion to Have
a Disputation with the Priests

AFTER THIS, THE MAHARAL WROTE a letter to the cardinal of Prague, Jan Salvester, requesting an invitation for a debate concerning the blood libel. He declared he was prepared to offer incontrovertible proof that this was fundamentally untrue and that it was just a despicable false accusation.

The cardinal responded that he agreed and was prepared to participate. A few days later, the cardinal summoned three hundred learned priests to the disputation. When the Maharal learned of this, he sent a message to the cardinal. Debating face to face with three hundred priests, he wrote, was beyond his strength. Rather, he suggested that the disputation should stretch over a thirty-day period. Each day, ten priests would submit their questions and claims to the cardinal in writing; and each day the Maharal would come to the cardinal with his written answers.

The cardinal was amenable to this. When the disputation began, and during the entire thirty days, all the Jews in Prague recited the complete Book of Psalms daily at dawn in all the synagogues and houses of study and fasted on Mondays and Thursdays.

6

The Disputation

MANY QUESTIONS AND CLAIMS were raised during this disputation pertaining to Judaism and Christianity, and it was all recorded—from beginning to end—in a voluminous book of history.

Above all, the disputation reached a pitch of excitement regarding the following five questions:

1. Is it true that Jews are required to use the blood of Christians for the Passover holiday?
2. Should Jews be blamed for the murder of Jesus of Nazareth?
3. Since Jews consider Christianity as idol worship, are they obliged, according to the tenets of Judaism, to hate Christians?
4. Why do Jews hate and display great hostility to an apostate and always lie in wait to kill him?

5. Why do Jews exult over all the other nations on account of their great Torah? Can't the other nations exult even more because they are good by nature and by birth, and hence they didn't have to be burdened with the heavy yoke of such a great Torah, for they have no need for it?

For the first question the Maharal presented incontrovertible evidence from the Bible and the Talmud that the Jews consider blood extremely abominable and impure. Blood is prohibited and abhorred even more than fat, and so all the more the blood of a human being which defiles even by proximity. Purity and cleanliness are deeply rooted in and fundamental to the Jewish religion. So how can a Jew even possibly consider using human blood for ritual purposes and for fulfilling a religious precept?

For the second question the Maharal replied that first of all only the Sadducees' sect, which worked hand in hand with King Herod and the wicked Roman authorities who ruled in Jerusalem, took part in the death sentence of Jesus.

The Roman hatred of Jesus of Nazareth was very great, for the Roman rulers considered Jesus a rebel against their government, one who sought to free the Jews of the Roman yoke by means of a revolt and war, and then be crowned as their king.

However, the real Jews, namely, the Pharisees and the Essenes, did not recognize Herod's kingship and had no desire to take part in this trial.

Second, the Maharal replied that anyone who seeks revenge against the Jews because of the unjust death sentence against Jesus of Nazareth is truly a heretic, an unbeliever who has no faith in Divine guidance, Divine Providence, and God's dominion in this world.

This may be better understood by means of a parable. A mighty king had an only son who had many enemies in the capital city. These enemies once falsely accused this son of insulting and defaming the honor of his father, the king. The son was then imprisoned. Because of his conduct the judges sentenced him to die by hanging.

His father, the king, clearly knew that all this was a lie, just a false accusation by his enemies. Nevertheless, the king remained silent and voiced no protest.

Later, the judges' deputies came to carry out the sentence and put the king's son, who had also been subjected to hideous torments, to death in the presence of the king. The only son pleaded with his father, the king, and said: "Save me, father.

Rescue me from the hands of these murderers, for you know the truth—I never insulted or defamed you." His father, the king, remained silent; he did not even say a word but watched the deputies murdering his son without cause. Moreover, the king did not contradict the deputies' remarks that they were doing this at his behest.

Now let us examine this matter. Who is more culpable in the death of the son—the judges who erroneously sentenced him to death for the sake of the king's honor, or the king, who knew the truth, and didn't even lift a finger to signal, Let him go, whereupon the son would have been freed at once? Without a doubt one can conclude that the king himself was responsible for his only son's death.

Now let us return to our subject. The moral of this parable is obvious to everyone. Christianity declares that Jesus of Nazareth was the beloved only son of God. So, then, if the judges, believing that the son rebelled against his father and disparaged his honor and his teaching, rendered an erroneous judgment, where was the father's compassion? The Bible states, "As a father has compassion on his sons." When the son pleaded with his father, why didn't he save him from that cruel death? The son was killed gratuitously—solely for his father's honor and for violating his commands and his teaching.

Now if we assume that his father was powerless to save him or that all this was done without his father's knowledge, we demean thereby his father's honor, for it is improper—indeed absolute heresy—to think thus of God.

Yet Christian doctrine holds that Jesus was obliged to suffer this punishment and experience this cruel death by the will and resolve of God his father—even though he committed no transgression whatsoever—so as to atone for Adam's sin, to the benefit of all adherents of Christianity, who will not have to suffer the scourge of hell after their death but will ascend straight to the Garden of Eden.

In keeping with this view, then, Jesus died by the will and resolve of God in heaven. And, surely, according to Christian doctrine, Jesus agreed and wished for this, just like Isaac the son of Abraham wanted to be sacrificed on the altar in order to accede to God's will.

According to Christianity's tenets, it is obvious that the death sentence of Jesus brought relief and deliverance and eternal benefits to all adherents of the Christian faith. Why, then, should the Christians blame the Jews for this? And why do they believe in taking revenge against them and repaying evil for good?

And even if the judges who sentenced Jesus to death did not have that beneficence in mind but only harm, they still can in no way be held culpable, for the judgment was handed down from heaven and their sense went askew when they mistakenly sentenced Jesus to death.

If Joseph the Righteous said to his brothers, "Although you intended to harm me, God intended it for good . . . for the survival of many people," then surely the Christian peoples should not seek revenge against the People of Israel on account of this. Joseph's brothers truly wanted to harm him and premeditated their deed because they hated him. But the Jews who sentenced Jesus to death had no selfish motives but acted only for the honor of God.

And if according to Christian doctrine the trial was tainted and erroneous, why do they believe that it was God-ordained to assure the survival of many people, all the adherents of Christianity? Hence, they have no basis for saying of the Jews, "You intended to harm me."

Then the cardinal asked the Maharal: "If so, then why

was Pharaoh punished with severe plagues when the Israelites left Egypt? For is it not written in your Torah, 'Israel is my first-born son'? And if the father saw his son Israel's suffering and did not protest, he obviously wished this to happen and so he ordained it in the Covenant of the Pieces. So why was Pharaoh punished?"

The Maharal responded to the cardinal: "But there is a great difference between one incident and another. For Pharaoh declared, 'I do not know the Lord,' and did not believe at all that Israel was enslaved to him only because of God's decree. Hence, he did not realize that by keeping the Israelites enslaved he was fulfilling God's decree, but his tormenting them was solely for his own benefit. He did this not only to the Israelites but to all the slaves in Egypt whom the Egyptians oppressed in perpetuity, declaring there is no God capable of saving them from their hands. And that is why Pharaoh deserved punishment and why God showed him His mighty hand—to inform him that He was the Creator and the Master and Overseer of the world.

"However, the judges who imposed the death sentence on Jesus did so only to fulfill the precepts of God's Torah, for they thought of him as one who was going to abrogate God's

Torah, and they involved themselves in this trial according to the laws of the Torah solely for the sake of God's honor and not for any benefit to themselves.

"Therefore, one can readily see that if it really was a tainted trial, the merciful divine father should have had compassion for his only son and informed the judges from heaven not to kill Jesus for insulting God's honor. For the truth is Jesus did not insult God's honor at all. But since you believe that this was truly the will of God and that His son Jesus also wanted this, you can in no way blame the people at whose hands this was done, for they were only emissaries in this matter."

The Maharal also answered the last three questions by means of a parable. He said: "Let us examine the actions of an earthly king and the manner in which he deals with his armies. Every king has royal advisors, ministers great and respected. He also has various branches of armed forces. They have officers over thousands, over five hundred, over one hundred. A simple soldier has to submit to and salute his officer who leads a one-hundred man unit. Similarly, that officer to a leader of five-hundred, and the latter to a commander of thousands, and so on—but all this is done when the king is not present. But when the king himself stands in all his honor and glory and inspects his troops, all of them are obligated—from the lowest to the highest rank—to submit to and salute no one but the king himself. And then if one of them has a request, he must turn only to the king. And if a plain soldier makes his request to the leader of a one-hundred man unit in the presence of the king, or if the salute he is obligated to give the king is offered to his unit leader in the presence of the king, that soldier has insulted the king's honor and will be brought to judgment for punishment.

"This may be compared to the armies of the world vis-à-vis the King of Heaven. According to Judaism, pagans are only those who do not direct their pleas and prayers to the One Creator but worship the hosts of heaven, the stars, and the constellations. The Talmud absolutely despises those pagans and considers them licentious creatures, not men. But people who address their pleas and prayers to the One and Only Creator, the Master of the Universe, are not considered pagans by the Talmud.

"Similarly, according to the Talmud, a Jew who converts to paganism forgoes his humanity and is considered licentious. But one who converts to a monotheistic religion does not forgo his humanity and is not considered licentious. He will merely be brought to judgment. Of his kind it is said, 'Even though he sinned he is still a Jew.' It is understandable, then, that the hatred the Jews bear against apostates to Christianity is not the hatred mentioned in the Talmud where that apostate is considered licentious and subject to persecution, a hatred natural toward someone who has betrayed his people and his roots.

"Take for example an earthly king who like all other kings has several kinds of armed services—infantry, cavalry, charioteers, sailors, and the royal guards, who are the most elite. Some kings also have an armed unit whose soldiers are dedicated to it from birth and have a special attachment to it. If a plain foot soldier flees of his own accord from his unit to another branch of service, even though it is part of the royal forces, he will still be treated as a traitor and deserter from the king's service, and will surely be punished.

"How much more so if a soldier from that unit that serves the king from birth spurns his special unit and flees to another branch of service. That soldier will shame and disgrace himself even more. In addition to punishment, he will be held a traitor by his family and his people and everyone will scorn and despise him.

"This may be compared to Jews who convert to Christianity. Although they are not considered pagans, they still will be despised and disdained by the Jews for betraying their people and kindred. Such hatred is natural even though it is not a religious hatred.

"As for the Jews feeling superior to all other peoples because of their Torah and declaring, 'You have chosen us from among all other nations,' there is no justification for other nations to be envious and hate Jews in their hearts for this and challenge them and complain about it.

"This too will readily be understood by means of a parable about an earthly king. In his capital city the king had two thousand soldiers from two different branches of the military—one thousand from each. The king placed a heavy burden on one of these units and imposed much work on them, both physical and mental. He spurred them on and adjured them with many oaths to devote themselves to their labors all day long. Upon the other thousand-man unit the king placed only a minimal burden and easy work. One day a quarrel broke out between the two units. The ones who labored hard boasted and exulted over the other unit and declared they were more privileged; only they should be considered the royal guard. This shows that the king chose them over the other soldiers to give them the yoke of work and education only because he understood that the other soldiers were not capable or trained for such work.

"Now the ones who had the light load gloated over the other group and said: 'Just the opposite. We alone are more important and privileged in the eyes of the king and only we are worthy of being called the royal guard. And the proof is that because the king loves us he didn't want to burden us with excessive labor, for he understood that we were upright men by nature and followed the correct path even if we were free all day long. But the heavy yoke of work and education was placed upon the other thousand-man unit because the king knew them to be unruly men who would learn to become upright only through work and education.'

"This argument reached the ears of the minister of war, who was in charge of all the armed forces. He sent his deputy to tell them not to quarrel, harbor envy, or hate one another, for such disputes were for simpletons and fools. On the contrary, both thousand-man units could boast and be proud of their assignment and declare that the king chose them above the other and loved them more. And so it should be. For by means of this each group will love its work and will faithfully fulfill its tasks.

"We can no longer decide which of the two groups is right, but some day it will become clear of its own accord by means of two conclusive signs. One is that in the future we shall see to which of the two groups the king will give a greater reward for its work; and, two, when the king will reveal himself during a trip to his country, we will see which armed unit will be chosen to share honors with him. And then we will know that only it can be called the royal guard.

"The moral of this parable is easily understood: the entire matter revolves around the relationship between the Jews and the other nations. And only in the future will all the people of the world recognize and know who is more privileged. But for the present all this envy and hatred is but folly and stupidity."

The thirty days of disputation passed. A different and interesting debate took place each day. The cardinal found the Maharal's responses on all thirty questions very satisfactory and he paid him great honor. Nevertheless, one priest, Thaddeus by name, who was known for his anti-Semitism, stood up virulently against the Maharal. The priest maintained that in any case many Jews, benighted in their thinking, believed it was a great religious precept to use the blood of a Christian for Passover, saying that this was a tradition handed down from their forefathers and that even if their rabbi would decree otherwise they wouldn't believe or obey him. So how could the Maharal take responsibility for these benighted Jews whose education was very rudimentary?

Naturally, the Maharal could not rebut these remarks decisively. The entire disputation was later recorded in a book that was sent to King Rudolf. The Maharal's comments, delivered with intelligence and understanding, pleased the king, who sent his deputy to the Maharal to prepare the rabbi for an audience with him.

7

"A Man Who Excels at His Work Shall Attend upon Kings." This Is the Maharal

ON THE FIRST DAY OF THE MONTH of Shevat, King Rudolf sent a canopied carriage to the Maharal, accompanied by two high-ranking ministers, who gave him an entry pass into the king's palace. The Maharal rode with them to the king's citadel where he was given a royal welcome. The king spent an entire hour conversing with him, but the Maharal did not reveal what they had discussed. Afterward the Maharal was sent back home with equally great honor. He returned from his visit to the king happy and of good cheer.

"As for now," the Maharal declared, "I was able to reduce our misfortune with the blood libel by more than half. But I have great confidence that with the help of the Creator, blessed be He, I will succeed in nullifying this calamity completely."

Ten days later, King Rudolf sent a decree to all the courts

prohibiting outsiders from being accused in any trial involving the blood libel, except for the man clearly identified as having committed the murder. Moreover, at every blood libel trial the rabbi of the city or the head of the Jewish community must be present. Furthermore, the judgment rendered by the court in a blood libel trial must be sent to the king for his approval.

Thereafter, the Jews were able to enjoy a bit of freedom, for the fear of the Maharal fell upon the Jew-baiters. But the plague of the blood libel had not quieted down completely. For if one of the common folk bore a hatred against a Jew, he schemed to lie in wait for him and cast a dead Christian boy into the Jew's domain and accused him of ritual murder. And how was it possible to exempt the Jew from punishment if he was subjected to this false accusation?

The man the Maharal feared most was the priest Thaddeus, an anti-Semite and Jew-baiter and a sorcerer as well, in whose heart jealousy and hatred burned against the Maharal. The priest declared he would wage a vigorous battle to have him exiled from Prague forever. Thereupon the Maharal secretly revealed to his students: "This is why I fear the priest Thaddeus, for he possesses the spark of the Philistine, Ishbi-benob, while I have within me the spark of King David, peace upon him."

As is well known, David was relentlessly pursued by that Philistine and was almost caught by him. That is why the Maharal decided to enhance his strengths and make them firm as a mirror of cast metal, which would enable him to fight his adversary, the priest, with all his might.

8

How the Maharal Created the Golem

THE MAHARAL ASKED A QUESTION during a dream, inquiring what power would enable him to fight his adversary, the priest. The answer came from heaven: "You will create a golem made of clayey loam and order him to destroy the evil tormentors of Jews."

The Maharal's reaction to this was that these words contain combinations of names through whose power one can always create a living golem from clay. He then secretly summoned me, his son-in-law Yitzchok ben Shimshon Ha-Cohen, and his illustrious student, Yaakov ben Chaim Sasson Halevi, and showed us the heavenly response he had received after his dream question. Then he passed on to us the secret concerning the creation of the golem from clay and dust of the earth.

"I want both of you to help me create the golem," he

said, "for in a creation of this sort, the four powers of the four elements—fire, air, water, and earth—are needed. I was born with the power of air, while you," the Maharal told me, "were born with the power of fire, and you, Yaakov Sasson, were born with the power of water. And so, by means of the three of us, the creation will be fully completed."

The Maharal ordered us not to disclose this secret to anyone and instructed us how to conduct ourselves during the seven days before the event.

In the year 5340 (1580), on the 20th of Adar, at four hours after midnight the three of us left for the Moldau River on the outskirts of Prague. By its banks we looked for and found an area with loam and clay, from which we made the form of a man, three cubits long, lying on his back, and then shaped a face, arms, and legs.

Then all three of us stood at the golem's feet, staring at his face. The Maharal told me first to walk around the golem seven times, beginning on the right side, proceed to his head and circle around it to his legs on the left side. He told me what combinations of letters to recite as I walked around him. And thus I did seven times. When I completed the circuits, the body of the golem reddened like a glowing coal.

Now the Maharal ordered his student, Rabbi Yaakov Sasson, to complete the seven circuits as well and gave him other combinations of letters. When his circuits were done, the fire departed, for water had come into the body and vapor began wafting from the golem. Then he grew hair like a man of thirty and nails formed at the tips of his fingers. After this, the Maharal began his seven circuits. When he was done, all three of us recited in unison the verse: "He breathed into his nostrils the breath of life and the man became a living creature," for even the atmosphere we inhale must contain fire, water, and air, which are the three elements mentioned in the *Book of Creation*.

Then the golem opened his eyes and gazed at us in wonder. Now the Maharal called to him in an insistent voice: "Stand on your feet!" Suddenly, the golem sprang up on his feet. Then we dressed him in the clothes we had brought with us, garb that was suitable for a shamesh of the court. We also put shoes on him. In short, he looked like the rest of us: he saw, heard, and understood, but he did not have the capacity for speech.

At six in the morning, before the break of dawn, four men returned home. As we walked back, the Maharal told the golem: "Know that we created you out of the dust of the earth to guard the Jews from all harm and from all the ills and troubles they suffer at the hands of their enemies and oppressors. Your name will be Yosef. You will live with me, sleep in a room in my court, and serve as the shamesh of the court. No matter where I send you, you will obey each one of my commands, even enter into a blazing fire, immerse yourself in deep water, or leap from a tower until you complete the task I have given you."

As he listened to the Maharal, the golem nodded like a man agreeing with his friend's remarks.

"I called the golem Yosef," the Maharal told us, "because I drew into him the spirit of Yosef Sheyda who is mentioned in the Talmud, a creature half man and half demon, who also served the sages of the Talmud and saved them a number of times from great calamities . . . Even if the golem enters a blazing fire," the Maharal added, "he will not be burned, nor will be drown in a river or be killed by a sword."

Regarding the golem, the Maharal told members of his household: "While on my way early this morning to the ritual bath, I met this poor mute on the street and marked that he was a great simpleton. I felt sorry for him and brought him home to help the shamoshim of the court. But I forbid members of my household to use the golem for domestic purposes."

And because the golem always sat in a corner of the court-room at the edge of a table resting his head on his hands, looking indeed like an unfinished vessel, lacking wisdom and understanding nothing and not worrying about a thing under the sun, the people called him Yossele the golem, while some named him Yossele the mute.

9

How Yossele the Golem Carried Water for Passover

BUT PERELE, THE MAHARAL'S WIFE, peace upon her, could not resist making use of Yossele the golem a day before Passover Eve to help her with holiday preparations. Unbeknownst to the Maharal, she motioned to the golem to fetch water and fill up the two large barrels that stood in a special room that had already been cleaned and made ready for Passover and into which no one entered prior to the holiday. Yossele quickly seized the yoke and the two buckets and dashed off to the well to bring water. But no one was around to notice what he was up to as he brought in the water. In short, Yossele the golem did not have the faintest idea when to stop fetching water.

Because no one told him to stop, he kept on bringing water and pouring it into the barrels, even though they were already full. The water now covered the floor up to the threshold. Then it began flowing to the other rooms. When members of the household noticed the water suddenly gushing on the floor of the house, they became frightened and astounded. "Water! Water!" they began shouting.

The Maharal too was frightened at their cries.

They looked and searched and when they opened the door where the two barrels stood they finally discovered the source of the water. There they saw Yossele the golem pouring the water. This prompted a great deal of laughter in the house and the Maharal too began laughing.

"Look here," he told his wife, "you found yourself some water carrier for Passover!" He immediately ran to the golem, took the bucket from him, and said, "Enough! That's quite enough!" The Maharal then brought him to the courtroom and sat him down in his place. From then on the rabbi's wife was careful not to make use of the golem for her own needs. Because of that incident, a popular saying spread through Prague. When someone wanted to criticize a workman's shoddy labor, he would say, "You're fit to be a watchmaker like Yossele the golem is fit for water carrying."

10

How Yossele the Golem Caught
Fish for Rosh Hashana

THE MAHARAL HIMSELF ONCE made the same mistake his wife, the rebbetsin, had made in using the golem to bring water for Passover. The rabbi used him to catch fish for Rosh Hashana, an incident that also ended in laughter.

Several years later, because of a great storm and freezing weather, there was a lack of fish in Prague for Rosh Hashana. The morning of the eve of the festival had already arrived and there was not a fish to be had in the city. This caused the Maharal such great distress he gave himself dispensation to use the golem and send him to catch fish for Rosh Hashana. "A task like this," he declared, "is considered a mitzva."

The Maharal, confident that the golem would catch fish even during a windstorm, provided him with a net and told him to go to the river and catch fish. Since the rabbi's wife had neither a small basket nor a small bag for the golem to store his catch, she quickly gave him a big wheat sack.

Yossele the golem took the net and the sack and ran off to the river despite the windstorm and the icy cold.

Just then someone brought a gift to the Maharal—a fish, not large but medium sized—from a village near Prague, which pleased the rabbi greatly. Because of this, people paid scant attention to the golem's assignment and did not await his return. Moreover, since they were busy on the eve of the holiday with Rosh Hashana preparations, they almost forgot about him.

Toward evening, at Mincha time, the Maharal had to see the golem and sent for him. "The golem has not yet returned from fishing," he was told. "Perhaps because it's hard to catch fish on account of the wind and the cold and he's afraid of returning empty-handed."

But since the Maharal had to see the golem urgently, he sent the old shamesh, Reb Avrohom Chaim, to summon the golem home at once. "If he says he can't return because he still hasn't caught any fish, tell him that the Maharal will forego the fish and that he can return home without them."

Reb Avrohom Chaim the shamesh went to the river and saw the golem standing in the water holding the fishing net.

While waiting on the riverbank, he told the golem from afar: "The Maharal wants you to return home at once."

The golem then lifted the big sack lying next to him containing fish and showed it to the shamesh. He indicated it was not full yet; in fact, it was far from being full. So how could he return home if the sack wasn't full of fish? The volume of the sack was the equivalent of ten bushels of grain. Reb Avrohom Chaim realized that one-third of the sack had yet to be filled. So he shouted to the golem and told him: "The Maharal said he'll do without the fish, but come back to him at once."

Hearing these words, the golem quickly grabbed the sack and shook out all the fish he had caught, sending them back to the water. Then he threw the net and the empty sack over his shoulder and ran back to the Maharal.

Later, Reb Avrohom Chaim too returned to the Maharal's house and reported everything the golem had done. At this, there was much laughter in the house. Then the Maharal whispered in our ears: "Now I see that the golem is fit only to save the Jews from various troubles and calamities, but not to help them observe mitzvas."

11

For What Purposes the Maharal Used the Golem

THE MAHARAL USED THE GOLEM only to save Jews from distress, and through him he performed many wondrous and miraculous deeds. Most of all, Rabbi Loew used the golem to fight against the blood libel, which was quite widespread during his time, and from which false accusation the residents of Prague and its environs suffered a great many calamities. Whenever the Maharal had to send the golem to a place of great danger, where it was not safe for him to be seen by anyone, he placed an amulet written on deerskin upon the golem, which made him invisible.

Every year, between Purim and the Intermediary Days of Passover, the golem was disguised in gentile garb each evening. No one could tell who he was, for he looked like a Christian porter and was girded with a rope belt just like the other porters. The Maharal ordered the golem to spend the night walking the streets of the city, especially those of the Jewish Quarter. If he saw anyone carrying something on his shoulder or transporting some bundle in a wagon, he was to rush toward that man and inspect him and his load.

If the golem saw that the object was the corpse of a boy who would be cast into one of the Jewish houses, he was to seize that man along with his burden, bind them with his rope belt, and drag them off forcibly to the Town Hall, where sat the police chief, police officers, and other city guards, in order to have that man arrested and brought to judgment.

12

The Maharal's First Miracle with the Golem

IN PRAGUE LIVED A VERY WEALTHY communal leader, known as the "primus," named Reb Mordechai Meisl, to whom a gentile butcher owed five thousand kroner. Reb Mordechai, a moneylender by profession, emphatically demanded a repayment of the loan. But since this butcher either did not want to repay his debt or was unable to, he came up with a wily stratagem: he would accuse Reb Mordechai of blood libel, for which the latter would be imprisoned, whereupon the butcher would cease being hounded to pay his debt.

In the city outskirts, a slaughterhouse used by both Christians and Jews stood by the Jewish Quarter, through which the gentile butchers delivering meat to the city would have to pass. Some days before Passover, a Christian child died in a house next door to the gentile butcher. As was the custom, the little boy was buried in the Christian cemetery.

After attending the burial, the butcher stole the child's body from the grave that night and then killed a large pig in the slaughterhouse. He scooped out the pig's intestines and put the child's corpse into it. He had previously slit the child's throat to make it seem that some human hand had slaughtered it. Then the butcher wrapped the child's body in a Jew's fringed prayer shawl to give the impression the Jews had done the deed.

That same night the gentile butcher placed the pig into his cart and made his way to the city through the Jewish Quarter. He stopped near Reb Mordechai Meisl's house, in order to cast the dead child into his cellar and thereby initiate a blood libel.

Now Yossele the golem saw the cart from afar and ran up to it. As he searched it carefully, his hands touched the pig and felt what was put into it. Yossele the golem then took his rope belt and forcibly began tying the butcher to the cart. But this butcher, no weakling either, began struggling with the golem, fighting to prevent the golem from tying him to the cart.

However, the golem's strength overpowered him and amid fierce blows he wounded the butcher in several places. Finally, the gentile butcher submitted to the golem, whose strength was supernatural. The golem then sat on the cart and quickly rode in it to the city's Town Hall to the office of the police chief.

The golem's cart, entering quickly and noisily, created a great tumult among the many policemen gathered in the Town Hall courtyard. A large group immediately surrounded the cart wherein the gentile butcher, bleeding from his wounds, was screaming in pain from the golem's unsparing blows.

The policemen untied the gentile butcher and pulled the injured man from the cart. Some ran to fetch a doctor to bandage his wounds, while others rushed to bring candles for light. Meanwhile, the golem fled from the scene and no one pursued him.

When the policemen kindled the lights, they searched the cart and found the pig. In its stomach they noticed the dead child with an apparently slit throat, wrapped in the prayer shawl of the Jews.

The police understood at once the matter before them and immediately began to intensively question the gentile butcher. At first he denied everything, but since his deceit was so obvious, he was forced to admit that he had not murdered the child but stolen him from the Christian cemetery in order to perpetrate a blood libel against Reb Mordechai

Meisl, who was pursuing him relentlessly to repay the money due him.

The police inquired: "Who brought you here forcibly, and who beat and wounded you?"

"A mute Christian porter suddenly ran toward me," the butcher replied. "By the look on his face and his great strength, he was a demon, not a man. He beat me and wounded me badly because I wouldn't let myself be tied up with his rope."

The Christian butcher was placed under arrest in the prison and brought to judgment.

The following morning this strange incident became known all over the city, but no one knew or understood the source of this great salvation. This incident struck terror into the hearts of the Jew-haters. Only the priest Thaddeus realized that no one but the Maharal could have done this with the help of a supernatural power. Therefore, the priest spread the word in the city that the Maharal was a sorcerer. His hatred of the Maharal increased greatly and he constantly thought of plots and schemes to contend with the Maharal and all the Jews of Prague.

13

The Astonishing Tale of the Healer's Daughter

IN PRAGUE THERE WAS A JEWISH healer named Mauritzi who, although estranged from Judaism, was still considered a Jew. He had a fifteen-year-old daughter who strayed from the straight and narrow path and was lured to convert out of her faith and become Christian.

One night, during the Intermediary Days of Passover, she ran away from her father's house to the infamous priest Thaddeus, who had a reputation as a virulent anti-Semite. He ceaselessly planned stratagems to spread a net at the feet of Jewish girls who would then fall into his trap and convert.

This incident was connected to another one that occurred in Prague. A Christian woman from a village near Prague had been a housemaid in the city for several years. During the winter, she was one of those who would kindle the Jews' ovens on Sabbath. Since she was always going in and out of their houses, she was well known in the Jewish community.

It so happened that after Purim a quarrel broke out between the maid and the family she served, whereupon she suddenly fled from her employer's house at night. No one knew where she had gone. Assuming the maid had surely run off to her native village, the family was not overly concerned about her departure and told no one about it. But no one knew exactly where she lived.

When the priest Thaddeus was informed that a Christian maid had disappeared in Prague, he decided to use this incident as a pretext for initiating a blood libel against the Jews of the city. And since he always secretly inquired and probed about doings in the Maharal's house, he learned that the rabbi had gotten himself a mute servant whom he would use to guard the Jewish Quarter against a blood libel. Therefore, the priest fabricated the accusation in a way that the Maharal's shamoshim would be caught and perhaps even the Maharal himself would be implicated.

It was at this time that the healer's daughter fell into the priest's hands and was prepared to convert. She lived at his place, locked into a secret room in the courtyard of his cloister. Then the priest enticed her with the following words:

"On the day the cardinal makes you a Christian, he will ask you why you are converting and what prompted you to do this—for it is customary to ask such questions—your reply should be: 'I'm doing this because I can't stand the cruel customs of the Jews who, according to their belief, slaughter a Christian every year and use his blood to mix it into the matzas they bake for Passover.'"

The priest also coached her to tell the cardinal that a few days before Passover she herself had seen the city rabbi's two shamoshim coming to her father's house one night.

"Tell the cardinal that one was an old man of short stature; the other was a young man of average height with a black beard who could not speak but only gesture with his fingers as do deaf mutes. They told your father that the city rabbi had sent him a flask of blood for Passover. Your father paid a lot of money for this blood, which was mixed into the dough of the matzas. And that is why you became terribly disgusted with eating matzas and with the entire faith of the Jews and decided to convert to Christianity."

The priest also taught her to say that, according to rumor, it was learned that the Christian maid who had disappeared had fallen victim to the Jews who had slaughtered her and taken her blood to distribute it among the Jews before the recent Passover holiday.

The day arrived when the healer's daughter's met with the cardinal, and it came to pass just as the priest Thaddeus had thought. The cardinal asked her the customary questions and she replied craftily just as the priest had instructed. She also asked the cardinal: "Do not implicate my father in this accusation, for he had nothing to do with this matter and would not want to be a witness in this case. You see, all the Jews of Prague are afraid of the rabbi of the city, who is considered a holy man by them and whose command they obey meticulously."

The remarks of the healer's daughter who had converted spread quickly through town like an arrow out of a bow and a great fear fell upon the Jews.

On account of this, the cardinal was obliged to submit a protocol to the court, even though he knew in his heart that this was just a false accusation. In any case, he could not hide this matter from the priest Thaddeus, who urged him to rush the protocol to the court.

After the protocol was prepared, the cardinal sent the Maharal a copy of its contents so he could devise a plan for the truth to surface. The malicious contents of the protocol showed that the priest Thaddeus had written it. The document declared that the apostate girl had testified to the cardinal that the Jews of Prague had mixed Christian blood into their matzas this past Passover; that from the rumor in town she had learned that this blood was from the gentile maid who had disappeared several weeks before Passover; that this blood had been distributed among the Jews by the Maharal's two shamoshim, who took a lot of money for it; and that the Maharal's hands too were no doubt besmirched by the blood of this innocent soul.

When the Maharal found out that this protocol had been sent to the court, he realized the first thing the court would do is order the two shamoshim seized from their beds at night and jailed, as was always the custom. Therefore, the Maharal decided upon the following course of action: he knew that this apostate girl was not familiar with Yossele the golem's face. And since the Prague poor never lacked raggle-taggle blind, deaf, mute, and lame people, he sent one of his resolute men to choose one deaf mute from among the poor who somewhat resembled Yossele the golem in height and age and bring him to the Maharal.

The Maharal's wishes were fulfilled.

When a deaf-mute who knew absolutely nothing of the events in town nor of the news on everyone's lips was brought before the Maharal, the rabbi said: "I want the golem hidden in a different house and have him stripped of his usual weekday garb and dressed in other clothing, and then I want the golem's clothing brought to me." Then the Maharal added, "And now prepare a fine supper with brandy for the deaf-mute and lie him down in Yossele the golem's bed in the room of the rabbinic court."

The deaf-mute was astounded by the honor accorded him and enjoyed immensely the fine food and brandy he had been served, the like of which he had perhaps never tasted in his life. Then he lay down and slept.

"Take the deaf-mute's clothing away," the Maharal instructed, "and replace it with Yossele the golem's clothing, which everyone recognizes as the garb of the shamesh of the rabbinic court."

In the middle of the night, the police surrounded the house of the old shamesh, Reb Avrohom Chaim. They entered his living quarters, took him from his bed, arrested him, and brought him to the prison. At the same time, other police surrounded the courtroom where the golem slept. Some of them entered and, assuming that the mute second shamesh lay on the bed, began to rouse him from his sleep. After much effort, they finally succeeded in waking the mute stranger, who was deep in a sweet and contented sleep.

When the deaf-mute woke, he saw policemen standing before him holding spears and swords. He was terror-stricken and did not know what they wanted from him. But the police signaled him to put on the clothing beside him. Frightened and confused, he did not realize the clothes were not his. He dressed and then he too was taken to the prison.

Morning came and Prague was in turmoil because of the terrible news concerning the accusation against the Maharal's two shamoshim. Everyone was afraid that the Maharal himself might be caught in this evil trap, God forbid. No one knew what to do. The only help they could offer was cries and groans and recitation of Psalms.

The trial was set for one month hence and the Maharal too was invited by the court to attend, according to King Rudolf's edict. But although the Maharal was neither tranquil nor composed, he did his best to be helpful in this matter. First, he ordered learned and zealous men to thoroughly investigate the home where the Christian maid had worked to discover where she was born and where her family lived, in order to know where to look for her, for she surely had fled to her hometown. They also probed assiduously the reason for her flight.

The inquiry suggested that the search for the girl focus on four places—two villages and two small towns only several kilometers from Prague. The Maharal took eight men and sent them secretly in groups of two to these four places, where they were to stroll about furtively and look for the runaway Christian maid.

Twelve days passed. When all eight messengers returned empty-handed, the Maharal was overcome with much anguish and grief. Three days later, the Maharal summoned Yossele the golem at night and asked him: "Do you know the Christian maid who used to light the ovens in Jewish houses on Sabbath?" Then he added, "Because of the girl's disappearance from the city a blood libel accusation has suddenly been leveled against the Jews."

Yossele the golem signaled that he knew the girl well and would even be able to recognize her among one thousand people. Thereupon, the Maharal wrote a letter to her in the local language in the name of the master of the house where the maid had been employed, requesting her to return to him.

The letter stated that he regretted the sin he had committed against her and the wrongs she had suffered of late in the house. After asking for forgiveness, he begged and cajoled her to come back at once and she would lack for nothing at his house. For this reason, he is sending her a special messenger, this mute, a member of his family, along with money for travel expenses and for hiring a special wagon to return immediately to Prague. Adding flattering remarks, he further urged her not to deny his request and plea, but rather hire a special wagon at once and return with the messenger to Prague.

In the letter the Maharal also sent sufficient money to enable her to have more than enough for travel expenses. Then the Maharal gave Yossele the golem the letter with the money. "This maid is surely in one of these four places," he told him. "Be quick and very persistent in your search for her," was the Maharal's strict order. "Walk around for several days in each town and look for her diligently until you find her. And when you do, give her this letter and the money and make sure you bring her back to Prague. In other words, don't leave her until she returns to Prague with you. And you must accomplish this mission during the two weeks before the trial begins."

The Maharal then dressed the golem in gentile garb and gave him food for the journey. Before dawn, the golem was already on his way.

The two weeks passed quickly. The day of the trial was near. Since Yossele the golem had not yet returned, the heart-broken Maharal decreed a day of fasting for all of Prague on the day before the trial. He also issued a proclamation for all the Jews to assemble at dawn in the synagogues and prayer houses on the day before the trial to recite the complete Book of Psalms with wails and weeping. In the Great Synagogue, the Maharal himself went up to the prayer stand to recite Psalms and the entire congregation wept with him.

On the morning of the trial, the masses—most of them Christians—started gathering in front of the tall building made of hewn stones and dedicated to great tribunals. Then the judges began arriving at the courthouse. The priest Thaddeus and the healer's apostate daughter came in a covered wagon. Then the two shamoshim, bound in chains and surrounded by many guards, were brought to the courthouse. The Maharal, accompanied by the head of the Jewish community, Reb Mordechai Meisl, arrived in a beautiful chariot.

The presiding judge rang the gold bell before him to signal the start of the trial. First, he turned to the old shamesh, Reb Avrohom Chaim. "Do you admit your guilt in distributing Christian blood among the Jews before Passover so they can mix it into their matzas?" the judge asked.

"I haven't got the faintest idea about any of this," the old shamesh replied.

Then the presiding judge took small flasks filled with a red liquid and asked the deaf-mute with gestures if he had carried such flasks.

The mute, assuming that those flasks surely contained red brandy and that the judge wanted to offer him a glass, nodded to indicate, Yes, yes. Joy and desire suffused his face as he put his finger in his mouth.

Then a roar broke out in the courtroom, for the priest Thaddeus had risen and addressed the judges: "This mute is an honest witness. He's indicating Yes to testify that it is true that he had had in his hands flasks of this sort filled with blood. That's why he put his finger in his mouth to show that it was this blood that the Jews had consumed."

The anti-Semites present agreed with the priest, but many in the courtroom laughed at this and declared that the deaf-mute's gesture of Yes indicated that he would willingly drink a glass of red brandy.

After this, the lawyer brought in by the defendants took a knife and, as the deaf-mute watched, passed it across his throat to indicate slaughter. He pointed to the Maharal and to the small flasks, asking by signs if he knew something of this matter.

The deaf-mute grew pale and shook his head to signify, No.

At this point, the priest Thaddeus said, "The deaf-mute assumed you were asking him if he wanted to slaughter the rabbi and that's why he said No."

When the defense counsel began to argue with the priest, the presiding judge rang the gold bell to silence the contenders. He then summoned the apostate girl to testify. "Don't be afraid of telling everything you know pertaining to this trial."

In a smooth-tongued manner, point-by-point, as recorded in the protocol and reflecting her testimony before the cardinal, she told the judges: "These two shamoshim brought the blood-filled flasks to my father by order of the rabbi. My father paid handsomely for this and put the money into the hands of this old shamesh. The flask of blood was held by the second deaf shamesh, from whose hand I myself took the flask to hide it, according to my father's wishes."

"How do you know that the Christian maid who disappeared is the victim whose blood this is?" the presiding judge asked.

"Because before the shamoshim left my father's house," she replied, "this old shamesh shook my father's hand as a mark of departure and said the following: 'Don't worry, Mister Mauritzi. When the cold of winter arrives, the One

Above will find us another victim to light our ovens on the Sabbath.'"

Now the defense counsel approached the apostate girl. "Do you know well the faces of the two shamoshim who visited your father? And are you absolutely sure they were the ones who now stand before you?"

"Of course it is they," the apostate girl answered with a laugh. "I would recognize them in the dark."

When the defense counsel saw she was impudently sticking to her story, he requested the judges: "Send for her father and bring him to the court to enable us to cross-examine him to see if his testimony coincides with his daughter's."

But the presiding judge answered, "Even before the onset of the trial, a letter was sent to the father, summoning him to testify as a witness. However, two weeks have passed and we have learned that the father has moved out of Prague altogether to a place unknown. Hence, it will not be possible to delay the trial over this."

When the presiding judge had completed his remarks, the sounds of tumult and noise of a shouting crowd were suddenly heard outside the windows of the courthouse. The people within grew alarmed and ran to the windows.

"What's going on?" they asked. "What's happening out there?"

They became aware at once that marvelous events were taking place outside.

This is what happened.

The real Yossele the golem had suddenly appeared, driving his wagon in great haste and dispatch into the crowd in front of the courthouse. In the wagon sat the very same Christian maid who had suddenly disappeared from her master's house and whom Yossele the golem had found in the village where she lived with her family. The letter with the money he had given her had worked to persuade her to return with him to Prague.

When the wagon had passed through the street where the Maharal lived, the golem stopped and jumped from the wagon to inform the rabbi that he had found the maid. He also wanted to change clothes. He removed the garb of the gentiles he was wearing and put on his Sabbath clothes, for his weekday clothing was now being worn by the deaf-mute stranger who was then in the courtroom.

Seeing that the Maharal was not at home and learning that he was in the tall stone building, the golem returned to the wagon, jumped into it, and himself began to drive the horses to the courthouse, right into the crowd gathered there. That is why a great tumult broke out in the crowd and loud shouts were heard. Some cried out, "Woe unto us!" mortally afraid that the horse-drawn wagon might run over them. Others emitted shouts of joy, especially Jews crying out a lusty "Hurrah!" for they recognized the true Yossele the golem and the Christian maid, and they realized that a miracle had occurred. That was the reason for their happy cries of "Hurrah!" and their applause.

Before long, the news reached the courthouse, which explained the tumult outside. The judges ordered the newcomers into the courtroom. As soon as the golem saw the Maharal sitting there, he jumped toward him. By means of odd gestures—which prompted a roar of laughter to break out in the courtroom—he indicated to the Maharal that he had found the missing maid and would show her to him.

But the priest Thaddeus and the apostate girl were terrified at hearing that the Christian maid had been found. The apostate girl fainted and fell to the ground, causing an even greater uproar in the courtroom, until they finally brought her to.

The presiding judge than rang his gold bell for silence

and order. He called the Maharal and sat him down in a chair beside him.

"Please tell us," the judge said, "who is this second mute man who brought the lost housemaid and where was she found?"

The Maharal then told the judges all about his laborious efforts from beginning to end to reveal the truth. "Everyone can see that this is a false accusation concocted by the healer's daughter, who is a traitor to her people and to her faith. I was helped by heaven to come up with clever ideas and good plans to save the lives of poor people, innocent of all harmful intent, from unwarranted punishment."

The Maharal's wisdom astounded the judges and his remarks amazed them. They immediately sent for the master of the house for whom the missing Christian maid had worked. When he entered the courtroom, he recognized her at once. The maid said she had run away because of the slanderous remarks that were being said about her. She also displayed the letter on whose account she had returned to Prague with the mute messenger.

At that point the presiding judge could no longer contain himself. He kissed the Maharal on the forehead and shook his hand lovingly. "We thank you for your efforts, your labor, and your wisdom, which has saved us from rendering a guilty verdict against innocent men."

The accused were immediately freed and in their stead the apostate girl was sentenced to six years in prison for perjury. The priest Thaddeus returned home humiliated and very furious, just as it is written about Haman, "his head covered in mourning," while the Maharal returned home happy and highly esteemed and the entire city of Prague too rang with joyous cries.

14

The Wondrous and Famous Story
Known as "The Daughter's Misfortune"

IN PRAGUE LIVED AN IMMENSELY wealthy and honored
wine merchant named Reb Mikhli Berger. Only in his cellar
were the choicest wines available and only from him did all
the priests and army officers purchase their wine. This merchant had a beautiful and intelligent sixteen-year-old only
daughter who managed the wine shop and supervised the
sale of wine, for she was fluent in several languages and could
deal with all kinds of people.

Even the priest Thaddeus, infamous as a vicious anti-
Semite, always bought his wine there. But he cast his evil eye
on this only daughter, who always sat in the shop. His plan
was to ensnare her and lure her to his house, where he could
entice her to convert to Christianity.

So adept was he in this sort of endeavor that a number of

Jewish girls had fallen into his net in this fashion. But with this Jewish girl he had no links or familiarity to enable him to drag her into his net, for she was truly a modest maiden of excellent virtue. Moreover, her parents were honorable, God-fearing people of distinguished lineage who watched over their only daughter like the apple of their eye: she wasn't even permitted to stroll outdoors on Sabbaths and holidays.

The priest hit upon the following ruse. He began buying wine on credit. This only daughter was in charge of the accounts book and recorded all the bills. After a while, she sent her servant to the priest with the bill that showed his debt. The priest paid in full. But his scheme was to create a dispute over the bill that would oblige the only daughter to come to his house with her accounts book to show him the error. And he succeeded in this stratagem, for the servant came several times with the bill and he paid it in proper fashion.

A few months later, when the servant was sent with the bill, the priest told him: "According to my accounts book this bill is wrong. You just want to take money unwarrantedly for ten more bottles of wine than is due you."

"It's not me who wrote the bill," the servant apologized, "but the winery owner's daughter."

"Then it is she who made a mistake in the bill," the priest

replied, "and when she comes here with her accounts book I'll show her the mistake."

The servant returned home with the bill and told the only daughter what the priest had said. Not suspecting anything amiss, she took the servant and the accounts book and both of them went to the priest.

When they arrived, the priest told the only daughter, "Your servant is demanding payment for ten additional bottles of wine, but I'm asking you to give me an honest accounting and to tell me how much I owe you according to your accounts book."

She acceded, but the second bill was still exactly like the first.

The priest marveled at this and, in so doing, pretended to recall something he had forgotten.

"I just remembered the bill is correct," he called out, "but I'm right too because some weeks ago ten bottles of wine were delivered to me that tasted just like vinegar and I didn't want to accept them. That's why they weren't written down in my accounts book."

This astonished the wine merchant's only daughter greatly, for she knew she always sent this priest the choicest wines. The priest then ordered his servant to go to the cellar and bring up the ten wine bottles that had been set aside in a special place in a separate basket.

When the wine was brought up, the priest told the only daughter: "I opened up only this one bottle that isn't full, and if you don't believe me, open another bottle and taste from it and you'll see it's vinegar, not wine."

She agreed to this. She took a bottle from the basket and ordered her servant to open it and pour a glass for her to taste. Now the priest had previously done something to ensure that all that wine would definitely be considered wine of libation. The only daughter never even imagined it was forbidden to drink this wine, even if it were just plain wine that now belonged to the Christians. When she tasted the wine she saw there was nothing wrong with it and she finished the entire glass.

"But this wine is perfectly good," she told the priest with a laugh. "What's your complaint about this wine?"

The priest feigned surprise. He also tasted the wine and declared: "It truly is a good wine."

And he ordered another bottle opened. The only daughter tasted first and noted that this wine too was good. Then the priest drank and said: "Now I see I was mistaken and you're right."

With this said, the priest, amid flattering remarks, began to ask pardon of the only daughter whom he had wrongly suspected and he took her hand in his and pressed it humbly and affectionately. Even though she had never before given her hand to another man, now she did not dare resist him and the wine of libation she had drunk helped her along in this.

"I have no ill feelings toward you," was her reply, "for all people are just flesh and blood and can make mistakes."

The priest then paid her all the money due her according to her bill and, with each exchange of conversation, spoke more fondly and amicably to her. As for the only daughter, drinking the non-kosher wine and shaking hands with the priest burned in her like a snake's venom and, feeling a change of heart, she began to enjoy the priest's remarks. She too engaged him in conversation and grew increasingly attached to him. When she left, she gave her hand to the priest of her own accord and parted from him with such affectionate words he felt he could invite her to visit him occasionally.

The priest's remarks were persuasive enough to corrupt her. From then on she began sending him letters by means of his servant who came to purchase his wine. He too wrote her letters and each time drew her closer and closer, until finally she secretly began visiting the priest by herself. This continued for a while until one time the only daughter did not come home to sleep but disappeared like a stone in water. A great commotion ensued and loud cries were heard in her parents' house, for they had no other children beside this only daughter.

The parents began to look for her and to probe and inquire of other people if they had seen her. Then a man informed them that he had seen her on the night she disappeared— walking through the narrow lane that leads to the priest Thaddeus' cloister.

This awful news grieved them bitterly; they understood that she was in dire straits if she had fallen into his snare. They ran to the priest in tears.

"Have pity on us," they cried out, "and return our daughter to us."

But the priest dismissed their pleas with laughter and even vented his anger at them.

"I haven't seen her," he said, "and know nothing about her."

Her parents returned home despondent, with tears on their cheeks. Everyone who saw them felt their great tragedy in their hearts.

The priest Thaddeus locked their only daughter in a secret place in the courtyard of his cloister where it would be impossible for anyone to see her or talk to her through a window. He saw to it that she didn't lack for anything. He visited her daily to discuss the Christian religion that she would be accepting and began to teach her the Christian prayers.

It finally dawned on the priest that the girl was sad and gloomy. Being alone had weakened her nerves, he concluded, and the only medicine for her pain was to find a suitable groom for her who would visit her from time to time, talk to her, and befriend her.

"Why are you so sad?" the priest asked her. He consoled her and said kindly, "You won't be alone much longer, for I'm arranging to find you a good and worthy husband whom you'll soon see."

Several kilometers from Prague dwelled an old and very rich duke who had an eighteen-year-old only son, good-looking, intelligent, and very learned. The priest Thaddeus was a dear and beloved friend of the duke and was considered a member of the family. He came up with the idea of marrying the duke's only son to the Jewish only daughter who lived with him in virtual imprisonment.

The priest visited the duke and mentioned his idea. He praised the only daughter exceedingly and told him her history. For them it was a great privilege to marry a Jewish girl who had converted to Christianity. The priest also persuaded the only son that it would be a feather in his cap if he would succeed in getting her hand in marriage.

The duke and his only son decided that after their customary Sunday visit to the Prague cloister they would remain to have lunch with the priest. He would then introduce the girl and if they liked her there would be consent all around.

On Sunday the old duke and his only son came to Prague and the priest prepared a great feast for them. When the wine had made their hearts merry, the priest sent someone to bring the girl to them. She already knew what was happening, for the priest had already told her previously to adorn herself and make herself pretty, as befitted the occasion, as today she would be called to present herself to a handsome intended groom. She did just that and appeared before them during the wine feast. Both the duke and his son liked her very much. That day the duke and his son did not return home but spent the night at the priest's residence to enable them to talk some more with the girl.

The next day the priest prepared another great feast. The girl was invited and sat joyfully next to the duke's son throughout the entire meal, just like groom and bride.

At the end of the banquet each gave a hand to the other

as a sign that the match was settled. They decided the wedding would take place two months later, on the very day just after the cardinal would officiate at her conversion to Christianity. The duke's son gave his fiancée a gold ring containing a beautiful precious stone, engraved with two letters, the initials of his name. They departed from each other with due deference and the duke and his son returned home.

But during all this time the girl's parents neither rested nor relaxed. With all their might they attempted to save their daughter from the clutches of the priest Thaddeus. However, all their labor was in vain. When her parents realized there was neither rescuer nor deliverer in their city, they decided to go to their kinsman, the great gaon, Rabbi Yaakov Gintzberg of the holy community of Friedberg, to save them from their woe, for the matter impinged upon him too.

"But in your own city," was the gaon's reply, "you have the head of the rabbinic court, the saintly gaon, the great rabbi, the Maharal! So why did you come to me? He can help you more than I."

Thereupon the gaon Rabbi Yaakov Gintzberg wrote a letter to the Maharal: "I earnestly request you to involve yourself in this matter and attempt with all your might to save the daughter of these unfortunate parents from the snare into which she has fallen, because this matter touches upon you too, for you are their kinsman and rescuer."

When the parents arrived at the Maharal's house, they immediately gave him the letter. They pleaded with him tearfully to save them from their great misfortune. The Maharal was terribly distressed by this letter and, knowing that the priest Thaddeus was a vicious anti-Semite and a vengeful and vindictive snake in the grass, he had no desire to enter into battle with him. But because of the great bond of friendship between them, the words of the great gaon, our master, Rabbi Yaakov Gintzberg, encouraged him.

The Maharal then decided to offer his assistance, but in order to prevent the priest from learning of his involvement in this matter he met secretly with his fellow townsmen. That is why the Maharal loudly proclaimed to everyone who had gathered in his house:

"I have no idea how to help these people and no desire to intervene."

At night, however, the Maharal quietly sent the old shamesh, Reb Avrohom Chaim, to summon the girl's distraught parents. Upon their arrival the Maharal told them: "I'm going to enter into this affair and find a solution for you—but in such a way that no one will suspect that I have had a hand in this matter. First, I want you to immediately prepare for tomorrow, in a hidden place in your yard, a covered wagon hitched to good horses and a good driver who is faithful and discreet. I also want you to get two other strong and brave men, friends whom you like and trust, who will be ready and willing to run off with the girl as soon as she comes home."

The Maharal also asked the parents: "Do you know of a safe place in another country to which you could flee with her and where she could stay peaceably and be cared for properly?"

"I have a very rich brother in Amsterdam named Reb Chaim Berger," the girl's father said, "and that will be a good place for her. He's a pious man, a Torah scholar, and he also owns the city's largest wine business."

This pleased the Maharal and he agreed that Amsterdam would be suitable.

"I want you both to fast for three days in a row, starting tomorrow morning," the rabbi told the parents, "and eat only at night. And on each of these three days, you will recite the entire Book of Psalms amid weeping."

The Maharal then sent them home, stressing absolute secrecy about their visit to his house that evening and his involvement in this matter. The unfortunate parents returned home, their hearts full of hope, and meticulously followed each of the Maharal's commands.

During these last three days in which the girl's parents fasted with prayers, laments, and tears, the girl in her room began to long very much for her parents. She imagined how they must be wailing for her and what wonderful parents they were to her—and now she had betrayed them and cast them behind her back to follow strangers. Unable to restrain herself, she cried all through the night, for she saw there was no escape for her soul from the trap into which she had fallen.

The next morning when the priest came to her, he saw her distress and noticed her red eyes.

"What's happened to you?" he asked.

"I'm feeling a bit ill," she replied, "but no matter, my indisposition will soon pass."

At that time the Cardinal of Cracow happened to summon all the priests under his jurisdiction to a large conference. Amazingly, the priest Thaddeus also attended, even though the cardinal was not his superior. Before leaving for Cracow the priest gave a strict warning to his servant not to let any stranger enter the cloister courtyard.

When the Maharal learned that the priest Thaddeus had gone to the priests' conference in Cracow, he secretly summoned Yossele the golem.

"A Jewish girl has fallen into the hands of the priest Thaddeus," he told him, "and she is surely in one of the secret rooms in the cloister courtyard. Therefore, I am now ordering you to rescue the girl from there tomorrow night and bring her to the house of her father, Reb Mikhli Berger."

That is why the Maharal adorned the golem with the well-known amulet that made him invisible. The Maharal also gave him a short letter that read: "I, your grandfather, have come from heaven to rescue you from this place. Hide in this sack and I will bring you to your parents."

The Maharal gave the golem a big sack and commanded him: "As soon as dawn breaks go to the cloister courtyard and stand next to the small iron door, for through it people enter and leave the courtyard. The door has the sort of lock that can also be opened from the inside even without a key. A stranger, however, will not know how to open it from the inside without a key unless he sees how it is done. Therefore, I want you to stand at that spot from early in the morning and wait until someone leaves. At that moment you will be able to enter without anyone seeing you, for the amulet has made you invisible.

"Once you succeed in entering," the Maharal also told the golem, "walk about the courtyard all day to learn well how to open the door from the inside without a key. Also look everywhere diligently until you find the girl's room, enter quietly, and hide there until after midnight. Once you sense that all the men in the courtyard are already asleep and the girl too is asleep, wake her and show her the sack and the letter. After she reads the letter, open the sack in her presence for her to enter it. Then take her on your shoulder, leave with her through the small iron door, and bring her to her father and mother's house. Then come back to sleep in my house."

The Maharal instructed him in all these details and warned him several times about each and every one until he saw that the golem had understood everything and was prepared to carry out all the orders.

Yossele the golem took everything he needed quickly early in the morning and went to the cloister, where he successfully accomplished all the Maharal had commanded him to do. Two hours past midnight Yossele the golem brought the girl to her father's house in the sack.

Who can describe and depict the tears of joy in the house when the unfortunate parents suddenly saw their only daughter standing before them. She fell to the ground at their feet and kissed them. Tears streamed down from her eyelids as she begged their forgiveness for the despicable deed she had done. Her father and mother fell on her neck and covered every part of her with kisses.

But when they asked her, "Who brought you here? Who was your rescuer and savior? Where is he?" she had no answer for them. She only showed them the letter the golem had given her.

"My grandfather from the supernal world came to me at night," she said, "and put me in a big sack, then fled with me and brought me here."

The father and mother believed this and thought that the Maharal had summoned him from the upper realm to come and save his granddaughter. But then the father remembered the Maharal's warning to flee with her at once to another country.

"Now is not the time to divert ourselves with our daughter," he told his wife, "nor to talk at length with her. Kiss her as much as you can for we now have to run away with her to my brother in Amsterdam."

All the preparations were soon made for this long journey. Reb Mikhli Berger, his daughter, and two capable friends climbed into the waiting covered wagon in the courtyard and they departed.

In the morning a great tumult was heard in the house of the priest's servant when he learned that the Jewish girl had fled. The servant was terror-stricken that the priest would hold him responsible for the girl's escape. We would never have known what ruse the servant came up with to avoid having the priest blame him for that occurrence, but from the story described after this one we can gather that the servant came up with this idea:

From the cloister cellar he took the bones of a dead man and placed them on the bed on which the girl had lain. Then he set the room on fire and before the firefighters could arrive the entire room was ablaze. The firemen found the burned bones of a man. A protocol was then written stating that in a room in the cloister courtyard a stranger who had come to consult the priest on a certain matter was found burned to death, and the guest's name was recorded in the protocol, as the priest later testified. And the next story after this one tells that the servant avenged himself on the priest and informed on him also regarding this matter: that the priest inveigled the only daughter of Reb Mikhli Berger and slyly enticed her to convert, forcibly locked her in a room, and tormented her until she lost the will to live and set the room in which she was imprisoned on fire.

When the priest Thaddeus came home from Cracow, saw the destruction, and heard the servant's remarks, he was overcome with horror. But he remained mute for he could not prove that the servant had lied. And so he was obliged to stay silent. In his heart, however, he knew that the fire could only have been set by his servant in order to cover up the escape of the girl. He suspected his servant of having been paid off to set the girl free and decided to get even with him, as will be seen in the next story.

The priest related to the duke exactly what his servant had told him: during the meeting of the priests in Cracow something terrible had happened in the cloister courtyard. Some hours after midnight a great fire broke out and spread to the room where the girl was sleeping and before the firemen arrived the room had become an inferno and only her bones were found.

When the duke's only son heard the awful news that his fiancée to whom he had been bound with bonds of love had been burned alive, he was exceedingly agitated and downcast. His depression led to a nervous breakdown, for his vivid imagination made him constantly see before him the tongues of fire surrounding the body of his beloved fiancée as she lay on her bed in sweet sleep then suddenly woke from her pains and could no longer battle the bitterness of death. Recalling this, his compassion was stirred for her and from that moment on he had no peace of mind. He neither ate nor slept; he was like a stunned man.

The old duke understood his son's illness and sought advice how to ease his distress. He entertained him with a variety of pleasant diversions and asked matchmakers to seek a proper match for his son, as befitted him. But nothing helped; no pleasure satisfied him; and no girl pleased him after experiencing the beauty, nobility of spirit, and fine character of the Jewish girl. Therefore he decided that his only consolation would be to take a Jewish girl for a wife, as refined and beautiful as his first fiancée.

But when the duke's son realized how difficult it would be to find a Jewish girl with all the good attributes—for it wouldn't be easy to find one willing to convert out of Judaism and accept Christianity, and perhaps he wouldn't even like the one who would—he hit upon the idea of traveling to a far-off land where he would convert to Judaism without his father's knowledge, study Torah, and then marry a Jewish girl of his choice, for money was no obstacle. And in order to have sufficient money, he told his father his plan.

"There is only one medication for my illness. As long as I

stay here I won't be able to forget my fiancée who was burned to death. And if this continues much longer I'll have no recourse but to be placed among madmen. And so here's my brilliant idea: I'll go to Venice to further my education and over several years get degrees from higher schools of learning. By concentrating all day on my studies in pursuit of higher education, I'll slowly and gradually forget my grief. Then I'll be able to return to your house, father, and seek another match."

Although the old duke loved his only son very much, and found it difficult to part with him for such a long time, he had no choice but to accede to his son's desire, for he truly feared for his psyche, lest his great grief lead him to madness. The duke thought that perhaps studying would hopefully make his son forget his anguish.

And so the duke gave his son as much money as he requested and sent him off to Venice. There the duke's son rented a private room and presented himself as a merchant who travels from land to land in pursuit of his business interests. He signed a contract with the landlord from whom he rented the room and said: "It's very likely I'll use the room only several times a year but I'll pay you an entire year's rent on condition that the room remains unoccupied and always ready for me. I have but one request of you. If letters come for me while I'm away, please take them out of the mailbox and put them into my room through the slot in the door."

All this the duke's son did in order to have an address for his father's letters and for him to reply to his father.

During that period the great and saintly gaon, Rabbi Yaakov Gintzberg, of blessed memory, of the holy community of Friedberg, was already world famous. In his day he was considered second only to the Maharal, for he too was a great scholar, well-versed in all the sciences and various languages. He was also the teacher of the man who wrote *Tosfos Yom Tov*. Therefore, the duke's son made up his mind to travel to the gaon Gintzberg, who would convert him and teach him Torah.

Upon his arrival the gaon took a great liking to him. Before long he converted the duke's son and gave him the Hebrew first name Avrohom and Yeshurun as a family name. The gaon Gintzberg himself studied Torah with the convert, Avrohom Yeshurun. And since he was widely learned and had a good mind, he quickly absorbed everything the gaon taught him. But because this gaon was very busy as rabbi and chief judge and head of the yeshiva in the holy community of Friedburg, he could not continue to teach the convert any longer. He sent him to the great yeshiva that flourished at that time in

Amsterdam and gave him a letter of recommendation stating that he was a good, decent, and sharp-witted fellow, and a kinsman as well. Therefore, the gaon requested in his letter that the head of the yeshiva give him lots of heartfelt warmth and watch over him diligently.

Avrohom Yeshurun parted tearfully from the gaon, our master, Rabbi Yaakov Gintzberg, who said: "I bless you with great success and also promise you that in Amsterdam a match worthy of you will be sent to you from heaven." The gaon gave him this sign: "When a match is offered to you and you are informed that the bride is of distinguished lineage and of the family of the gaon Gintzberg, I want you to know that this is the right match for you and that the bride is your destined intended. I also advise you," the gaon continued, "to keep the fact that you're a convert absolutely secret. Just say that you're from Bucharest and that your name is Avrohom from the Yeshurun family and that you're a kinsman of the gaon, our master, Rabbi Yaakov Gintzberg from Friedburg, which fact can readily be verified with the rabbi of the holy community of Friedburg."

Avrohom Yeshurun traveled to Amsterdam and came to the gaon, the head of the yeshiva, and introduced himself. He also showed him the letter of the gaon of the holy community of Friedburg. The gaon immediately welcomed him with heartfelt warmth and began to teach him Torah, which Avrohom Yeshurun studied with great diligence and acumen. He achieved great fame as a Torah scholar and became known as the Young Genius of Bucharest.

During this period he kept traveling to Venice to collect the letters his father, the old duke, had been sending him and to reply to them, so that his father would assume he was really living in Venice, studying in institutions of higher learning to complete his course of studies.

Avrohom Yeshurun studied two years in the Amsterdam yeshiva. The head of the yeshiva then ordered him to return to the city of his birth and marry a Jewish girl.

But he replied: "It seems to me Amsterdam is a better place to live because its people are God-fearing and scholars of Torah, the sort that can't be found in Bucharest. So I prefer to take a wife in Amsterdam and establish my residence here."

Avrohom Yeshurun also let it be known that he would offer as high a dowry payment as was requested of him, for he had no lack of money. And his father would send him however much money was needed for a fine match because he was a man of great wealth and he was his only son.

This news of the rich yeshiva student spread quickly throughout the city. The matchmakers began suggesting various matches to him, which he dismissed with flimsy excuses. Finally, one matchmaker suggested a match with the girl who was living at the wealthy Reb Chaim Berger's house. It was known in Amsterdam that she was an orphan, the daughter of Reb Chaim Berger's brother, and that she was heir to a great fortune. And since she had no one to live with in her hometown, she sought shelter in the house of her uncle, who would be her pillar of support.

Among her other attributes, according to the matchmaker, was her prestigious lineage and familial ties, for she said she was a close relative of the great gaon Rabbi Yaakov Gintzberg of Friedburg. Upon hearing that this bride was close to the gaon, Avrohom Yeshurun realized that the rabbi had made his prediction pertaining to this girl by means of his divine spirit and that she was surely his intended bride. He told the matchmaker that this match appealed to him and ordered him to pursue it.

Naturally, the matchmaker did not have to work too hard to complete the match, for there were excellent attributes on both sides. They only deceived each other on the matter of familial lineage. The groom fooled the bride regarding his birth, for he did not want it known that he was a convert and not of Jewish stock. And the bride fooled the groom and the entire city of Amsterdam regarding her birth, for she did not want it known whence she had been brought to this place, for she feared that the bad reputation she had had in her hometown for seeking to convert would become known.

In short, the match was arranged successfully, and the engagement contract was signed amid great splendor, even though it seemed to the groom that the bride looked familiar. However, it did not dawn on him that she was his first fiancée because her death in the fire in the courtyard of the priest's cloister had already been engraved in his mind.

Some weeks after the engagement, and before the wedding, the groom bought expensive gifts for his bride, including two gold rings set with precious stones. When the groom presented these gifts to his bride, she tried them on in his presence. But in order to place the rings on her fingers she had to pull off the ring she was already wearing. When she placed her old ring on the table, the groom picked it up and recognized at once that this ring had once belonged to him—one he had given the fiancée who had died in the fire. For besides the other signs the duke's son had noticed on the ring, he also saw the two letters engraved on the ring—the initials of his name.

A pall of great fear came over the groom. His heart melted within him and he fell to the ground in a faint. At once a tumult ensued. Some people tended to him, woke him, and brought him to. Soon he felt well again but he did not want to reveal the true reason for his fainting spell.

He then scrutinized his bride very carefully and assiduously studied her voice and each of her gestures until he gradually came to realize more and more that his present bride was the very one to whom he had been engaged in Prague. He could no longer contain himself and adjured her softly: "Tell me truthfully who you are and how you came to possess this ring . . . And don't have the slightest fear of telling me the truth," he added, "for no harm will befall you on account of this."

When the bride heard these words from him, she too became very frightened and fell to the ground in a dead faint, unconscious. The groom cried out, shouting for help. People ran to him, tended to the girl, woke her, and brought her to as they had him earlier. But she could no longer hide the secret she harbored within her and was obliged to reveal to the groom all that had happened to her. And now the groom could no longer restrain himself and, in a voice full of tears, began to speak to his bride: "I want you to know, my dear, that I am your first groom, the son of the duke, but now I am a Jew, just like all other Jews, and Divine Providence has guided me over the paths of the seas to come to you and cling to you."

Both of them shed bitter tears and each consoled the other and they rejoiced in newfound happiness and newfound love. Afterward, the groom revealed the entire secret from beginning to end to the gaon, the head of the yeshiva, with whom he had studied. The entire matter also became known to the bride's uncle, Reb Chaim Berger, who expressed great joy. But they were absolutely delighted when they heard the blessing given to the groom by the gaon, our master, Rabbi Yaakov Gintzberg, of the holy community of Friedburg, who had told the groom that he would find his match in Amsterdam. And regarding this, the gaon, the head of the yeshiva, remarked: "Now we can see with certainty that this is a match made in heaven. What the Evil One sought to accomplish by forbidden means—Divine Providence has turned around to make it permissible . . . Now go and enjoy your acquisition."

Soon thereafter the wedding was celebrated in Amsterdam amid great splendor. During that same year the old duke died and all his wealth, his estates, and all his villages were inherited by Avrohom Yeshurun. He and his wife settled in the father's estate in a big castle located in a village several kilometers from Prague.

When Avrohom Yeshurun and his wife moved into his father's estate, the priest Thaddeus was no longer in Prague, for he had been exiled and sentenced to hard labor for being found guilty in the murder of his servant's son for the purpose of the blood accusation, as can be seen in the next story.

Several days later, when the castle was kashered, Avrohom Yeshurun prepared a great banquet and invited his father-in-law, Reb Mikhli Berger, and his wife and a few friends. He also invited the Maharal and sent an elegant and beautiful covered carriage for him. Until now the mystery of who had rescued the daughter of Reb Mikhli Berger from the cloister courtyard had not been solved. But during the party each person began telling of the events of this marvelous story, narrating a bit of what he had experienced.

Then the Maharal said, "Because I was helped by Heaven to get rid of my evil opponent, the ruthless priest Thaddeus, I am no longer afraid of revealing the truth to you now. Know that it was not her grandfather from the world above who came to rescue the girl, but it was I who sent her a man carrying a big sack. And the little letter she got was written by me so that she would immediately obey and enter the sack."

All the guests applauded and were very happy with the Maharal's remarks. They thanked the Creator for the wonders and miracles He had done for them. The Maharal was given precious gifts, among them the covered carriage with the horses that had been sent to bring him to the castle. In addition, the Maharal was presented with much money for good causes and to establish charities in Prague.

Some years later Reb Mikhli Berger and his wife died, but Avrohom Yeshurun did not want to inherit his father-in-law's property, so he donated his house to the bes medresh which is why it is called the Yeshurun Kloyz. Besides this Reb Avrohom Yeshurun performed many other acts of kindness and distributed vast sums of money to charities in Prague. He lived many years with his wife, and achieved great success.

15

A Very Amazing Tale About a Blood Libel by the Priest Thaddeus Which Caused His Final Downfall and His Banishment from Prague

THIS AMAZING INCIDENT TOOK place in the year 5345 (1585). In Prague, opposite the Great Synagogue stood a very old and tall building that looked like a king's palace from bygone days. It was known as the Five-Sided Palace because of its pentagonal shape. Each of its five walls faced a different street and each wall had five tall, thick pillars made of hewn stones. Five large, wide windows were set between the pillars, and on the roof stood five tall towers which had carved images, indicating that this palace was built when people still worshiped the sun. And because everything on this building was connected to the number five it was called the Five-Sided Palace.

This palace did not have one owner; rather it was considered part of the properties and chattel of the government. And because the authorities did not want to spend any money for maintenance, the building continually fell into greater disrepair. For the most part poor people and indigent workingmen lived there.

Under this building ran long, spacious, cave-like cellars. But the tenants feared entering the cellars, for word had it that satyrs danced there and demons had taken possession of the place. By hurling stones and creating a storm wind they cast a pall of fear and dread upon anyone who wanted to enter. People said that more than one person was hurt when he sought to enter the cellars. Therefore, few tenants lived in that building.

In any case, as time passed the house became more and more dilapidated until it looked like an old ruin.

Once, before Passover, after the search for leaven had been completed at the Maharal's house, an incident occurred. The old shamesh, Reb Avrohom Chaim, was standing next to the Maharal holding a lit candle. Just as the Maharal was about to recite "All the leaven . . ." the candle was suddenly extinguished.

The Maharal had a custom of never saying anything by heart but always using his Siddur. He once told us that his custom was not out of strictness, but only because—based on the color of the letters in the Siddur—Heaven revealed future events to him, for there are colors that signify lovingkindness, while some signify judgment and others compassion, and the letters in the Siddur change to the color of the overriding attribute. One time, while reciting the *Avoda* portion of the Yom Kippur service, the Maharal burst into bitter tears. At the end of the holiday we asked him why he had wept and he explained to us that the same sign of the crimson thread used in the Holy Temple that turned white was also in the *Avoda* section of his Siddur. But this Yom Kippur the crimson letters did not turn white, for heaven had leveled a great accusation against the Jews. This caused the Maharal great grief, but his weeping mitigated somewhat the severity of the judgment.

That is why the Maharal gestured to the shamesh to kindle the light for he thought it a happenstance. The shamesh tried to light the candle a few times but still the wick sputtered and refused to light. The Maharal's face became white with fear, for he understood at once that the matter was not simple. All the people who stood there were also terrified. The Maharal was obliged to stop. "Take the Siddur and come with me to the candle burning in the wall lamp," he told the shamesh, Reb Avrohom Chaim. "Recite from the Siddur the paragraph 'All the leaven . . .' word for word in a loud voice and I'll respond by repeating the passage word for word by heart."

This the shamesh did. Confused and frightened by this incident, he approached the wall lamp, and began to recite "All the leaven." But when it came to saying the words "in my possession," it seemed to him that the words "in the five" were written in the Siddur. So he said out loud for the Maharal to hear: "In the five."

The Maharal did not repeat this but shouted, "Nu, nu!"— a hint that the shamesh had erred.

But the shamesh grew even more confused and began to say a second time, "All the leaven that is in the five . . ."

The Maharal then snapped his fingers as was his wont when something astounding had occurred. "That's it!" he cried out in a loud voice. "Now I understand that this is a time of trouble for Jacob and they seek once more to extinguish the Light of Israel. Now I also understand the interpretation of the dream I dreamed on the Friday night of the Great Sabbath."

The Maharal then rushed in a fright to the candle burning in the wall lamp. Because the lamp was set high the Maharal himself stood on a bench holding the Siddur up to the candlelight and recited the words to "All my leaven . . ." from the Siddur properly. When he finished, he ordered all the people who were in his house who lived in town to return home at once. Now no one was left in the Maharal's house except his son-in-law, the gaon, our saintly master Rabbi Yitzchok Katz, of blessed memory, the old shamesh, Reb Avrohom Chaim, and the other shamesh, Yossele the golem.

Then the Maharal related a terrifying dream he had had on the Friday night of the Great Sabbath: flames and fire were coming out of the Five-Sided Palace because of a great conflagration there. And he saw in his dream a huge tongue of fire leaping out of the Five-Sided Palace and breaking into a window of the Great Synagogue when it was full of Jews praying. He was very frightened in his sleep and began shouting at the top of his voice until he woke, afraid and terror-stricken.

"Now I understand the meaning of the dream," said the Maharal. "In this Five-Sided Palace an accusation and great misfortune has been planned for the citizens of Prague and we must quickly rid ourselves of it just as we rid ourselves of leaven. And that is why Heaven ordained that the shamesh, Reb Avrohom Chaim, should say the words 'All the leaven in the five' to remind us that we must get rid of the leaven in the

Five-Sided Palace where a trap and snare have been set for the citizens of Prague, for a fire has come out of the Five-Sided Palace and burnt the windows of the Great Synagogue when all the Jews were in it. And the fact that the candle was extinguished hinted that they want to extinguish the Light of Israel and that the misfortune was planned also against me, who is called the Light of Israel because I contain the spark of King David, peace upon him, who was also called the Light of Israel."

The Maharal began to probe and inquire how evil against the People of Israel could be found in the Five-Sided Palace. He himself asked about all the tenants who lived there—who they were and what they did. However, the old shamesh remembered each one perfectly and knew each one of the tenants well. He recalled each one's name and not one of them could be suspected of evil intent. For only poor Jews and simple artisans lived there. But one matter extremely agitated and frightened the Maharal.

"When I was a boy," the old shamesh told him, "the first-graders would tell each other old legends about the Five-Sided Palace, and everyone related what he had heard from his forefathers. One of these legends was that in ancient times a king lived in this palace who never showed his face to the people of the city. When he had to attend prayer services in the cloister, he went from his residence to the Green Cloister through a subterranean passage that was built from the cellar of the Palace to the cellar of the Green Cloister. And that Green Cloister is the very one where the priest Thaddeus, the bitter enemy of the Jews, now resides."

When the Maharal heard this legend he said, "If that is so, then this priest, who is my opponent and foe, has surely prepared some evil design in the cellar of this Five-Sided Palace, for he no doubt knows about this subterranean passage and it is easy for him to implement his plot without any interference."

The Maharal knew that this priest always lay in wait to crush him and have his vengeance upon him. The priest created wily stratagems to make him fall into the pit he had dug regarding the blood libel because the Maharal attempted always with all his might to guard the city from the false accusation of ritual murder. The rabbi also knew that the priest Thaddeus still burned with rage over the matter of Reb Mikhli Berger's daughter, because his scheme for converting her was thwarted. Moreover, this priest was a great sorcerer and understood that this could have been accomplished by no one but the Maharal; that the girl was stolen from her cloister room; and that the fire was purposely set by the priest's servant in order to camouflage the event. And from the remarks made by the priest Thaddeus, who justified himself afterward in the court before the judges, he seemed to assume that while he was at the priests' conference in Cracow his servant had taken a large sum of money in exchange for returning the girl to her parents. The priest also assumed that all this was done at the advice of the Maharal, which is why he decided to take vengeance against both his servant and the Maharal.

Indeed it was true that a terrible blood accusation had been planned against the notables of the city and also against the Maharal himself. Here is how it happened:

The priest Thaddeus employed a servant who had a wife and children. The priest's house stood in the courtyard of the Green Cloister. On one side of the house the windows faced the cloister courtyard; on the other, the windows looked out at a large garden surrounded by a wall with an iron gate that opened onto a road outside the city.

Two weeks before Passover, at the onset of spring when the trees were blooming, the priest's servant and his wife would go out in the afternoon to work several hours in the garden, hoeing the soil and trimming the trees. Their children would then begin to play in the garden and run around. While tend-ing the garden they opened the iron gate to throw away the refuse that had been collected in the garden throughout the winter. The servant's children would often run out of the gate and play there. In the evening, when the priest's servant and his wife returned home, they would call the children, who were scattered in the garden and outside of it; they would look for them and bring them home. The priest Thaddeus was aware of all this and thought this a good opportunity to take revenge against his servant and create a blood libel against the Maharal.

He lay in wait for the servant's children toward evening, at the time when their parents were busy with their work. The children were scattered in the garden and outside of it. Seeing one of the boys separated from his brothers and playing by himself near the priest's house, by deceit the priest lured him to his house. He took him to the big cellar, slaughtered him, and drained his blood into a vessel. Then he poured the blood into many small flasks and pasted labels on them with the names of notables in the city in Hebrew letters, including those of the Maharal, his sons and sons-in-law, and the three communal leaders who were called "primus." The priest brought all this from his cellar to the cellar of the Five-Sided Palace.

He also carried the body of the slaughtered boy there.

After passing through the subterranean passage that linked the two cellars, he placed everything into an old closet that stood in the cellar.

The priest prepared this great blood accusation so that he and the municipal police would be able to attack the Jewish Quarter on the Eve of Passover and initiate there a wide-ranging search until the accusation would be realized and he could arrest the Maharal himself along with members of his household and the notables of the city.

All this was done on Friday night of the Great Sabbath. And that is why on that night the Maharal had his terrible dream that was described earlier.

In the evening, the priest's servant and his wife had finished their gardening work and were about to return home. As they began to gather their children to go back home with them they noticed one boy missing. They looked for him till nearly midnight and could not find him. In the morning, the priest's servant and his wife came to the priest and told him what had happened to them.

The priest replied, "I think the boy surely ran off to play on the road outside the iron gate and got lost in the field." Then he added, "But there is something else you have to fear.

Since this day is close to the Passover holiday of the Jews and they lie in wait every year to slaughter a Christian and take his blood to mix it into their matzas, so who knows if the boy hasn't fallen victim at the hands of the Jews? Now you have no choice but to report this matter to the chief of police and ask him to quickly search all the Jewish houses."

The priest also advised his servant's wife: "Tell the police chief that on the day your son disappeared you looked through the iron gate toward evening and at a distance you saw a Jew in the field carrying a sack on his shoulder with something in it. Tell him the sack moved on his shoulder as though something living were inside it, and no doubt this Jew kidnapped your son for slaughter."

And the priest further ordered her: "Weep bitterly and fall at the police chief's feet and beg him to initiate the search as quickly as possible. Also ask him to have the priest Thaddeus accompany the police to help them during the search."

Hearing the priest's words, the unfortunate mother burst into tears and ran at once to the chief of police. She fell weeping at his feet and told him everything the priest Thaddeus had instructed her to say.

And then she added, "Start the search immediately with the help of the priest Thaddeus."

"I'll do everything you've asked me," the chief replied, "but it won't be possible to do this today because I must first obtain the consent of the mayor. I'll make the request today and tomorrow morning I'll start the search with the help of many men and accompanied by the priest Thaddeus."

Then he warned the woman, "But do not reveal anything about this matter to anyone."

It is written, however, "The Guardian of Israel neither slumbers nor sleeps." When Heaven revealed to the Maharal that misfortune was approaching which he had to eliminate like leaven and that this trouble was located in the Five-Sided Palace, he neither rested nor was he still. The Maharal girded his strength at once for a vigorous battle to eliminate this leaven.

"It is true," said the Maharal, "that it's dangerous to enter the cellar of that ruin. But I will rely on the Talmudic adage, 'No harm befalls those who are sent on a pious mission.' But even though people say it is a place where danger is to be expected, the merit of the Jewish multitude will protect me from all harm."

After midnight the Maharal took three thick Havdala tapers and a tinderbox. He gave one to each of his two shamoshim, Reb Avrohom Chaim and Yossele the golem, while he held the third. He also took his staff with him and all three walked silently into the Five-Sided Palace so that no one would be aware of them.

Arriving at the steps that led into the cellar, they lit the three tapers and continued walking. But when they opened the door, a blast of wind came and the cellar was filled with dust from the strong draft that extinguished all three tapers. They also heard many dogs barking and a great fright came over them.

"Don't be afraid," the Maharal told them, "but gird your strength and don't move." After the Maharal and Reb Avrohom Chaim repeated three times. "O You who dwell in the shelter of the Most High . . .," the wind and dust ceased and the dogs' barking subsided too. But as they walked further stones from the abandoned cellar fell on them. They feared that the vault of the cellar would collapse on them.

"Go you alone," the Maharal told Yossele the golem. "for even the demons won't harm you. Look carefully in all the rooms and if you find anything suspicious in connection with the blood libel bring it to me."

The Maharal and Reb Avrohom Chaim moved back to the door; only Yossele the golem proceeded forward by himself holding the lit Havdala taper. After looking he found a little basket with the slaughtered boy in it, wrapped in a fringed prayer shawl, and another basket containing about thirty small blood-filled flasks. Glued onto the flasks were little notes with the names of the Maharal, his son and sons-in-law, and other community notables.

When Yossele the golem brought all these to the Maharal, the rabbi commanded: "Take the slaughtered boy as is and carry him through the subterranean passage to the cellars of the priest Thaddeus's cloister. Look for the priest's wine cellar and hide the boy there among the barrels, well out of sight. Then come back to me using the same passageway."

The golem fulfilled all of the Maharal's orders flawlessly and returned half an hour later from the passage. The Maharal then told his two assistants to dig a hole in the cellar floor where they smashed all the blood-filled flasks with stones. They threw everything into the hole and covered it with earth so that no trace was discernable. After this was done all three men returned home happily. The Maharal commanded them not to tell a soul about what they had seen.

On the Eve of Passover at ten in the morning, the police chief suddenly appeared in the Jewish Quarter, accompanied by many policemen and soldiers. The priest Thaddeus had come along with them too. The soldiers and the police quickly barged into the homes of the Jews in groups of two and conducted a thorough search. The police chief and the priest Thaddeus first searched the Great Synagogue and then the Maharal's house and the houses of the community notables.

When they passed the Five-Sided Palace, the priest told the police chief: "This place should also be searched, for most of the time the Jews commit their ritual murders in ruins like this."

And so they also searched all the rooms of the cellar but they came back as empty-handed as they had come. In the afternoon they returned to their homes having accomplished nothing.

During the search a pall of deathly dread fell upon the Jews of Prague. But the Maharal immediately declared: "Tell the people in my name to pass the word not to have the slightest fear, for the trap has been broken and we have fled to safety. Now prepare for Passover with great joy, for the Rock of Israel and its Redeemer has performed hidden miracles for us to save us from false accusation."

For several days the body of the slaughtered boy lay well-hidden in the priest Thaddeus's cellar until it began to smell. Since the Christian Easter was approaching, about a week before the holiday the priest told his servant: "Go down to the cellar, clean it, and make order—and take inventory of all the wines so I can know how much wine to order for Easter."

The servant went down to the cellar, followed by the dog that always ran after him. As the servant began his work the dog scampered to and fro in the cellar, sniffing in every corner, as dogs are wont to do when they look for something.

Finally, the dog sniffed out the place where the dead boy was hidden. The dog then began to bark lustily and to dart back and forth on that spot. The servant, realizing this was not a trifling matter, began to search in that area until he discovered the boy's corpse. At once he saw it was his missing son. Terror-stricken, he ran to the police chief and told him what he had seen. The police chief, accompanied by soldiers, came quickly and went down into the cellar and saw that the servant had spoken the truth.

"This has to be the work of the priest Thaddeus himself," the servant shouted. "He always aspires to attack the Jews and provoke them with the accusation of ritual murder."

Everyone knew that the servant was absolutely right. At first the priest tried to deny everything, saying, "I know nothing at all about this matter." However, through several signs and wonders his crime became evident and the priest had to confess that his hands had spilled this blood—but he justified himself by stating: "I committed this murder out of zealousness for the Christian faith and because my servant robbed Christianity of a precious soul who had lived with me for several weeks. But then, in exchange for a bribe my servant took from them while I was away at a priests' conference in Cracow, he brought her back to her parents."

Then the priest added, "I also did it to take revenge against the rabbi of the Jews whose idea it surely was to bribe my servant. And that's why I killed his child—to incite a blood libel against the rabbi, in order to have my revenge against both of them."

But the servant threw the priest's denial back in his face. "Not so! You sneakily lured the daughter of Reb Mikhli Berger to you. You forced her to convert and you imprisoned her. And because of the depths of her suffering she grew sick of living and set her room on fire."

The matter ended with the priest Thaddeus' arrest and trial. His punishment was exile to an uninhabited land for the rest of his life. So may all the wicked enemies of Israel perish.

Regarding this incident, the Maharal created a humorous play on words. "When the Saturday night table hymn mentions 'protecting the esteemed woman,' this refers to the holy Shekhina; 'as well as the children'—that means the Children of Israel. 'Five, said the woman to him'—which means that by making the shamesh say 'five,' the Shekhina was sending me a message to carefully search the Five-Sided Palace, and eliminate the leaven—that is, the impurity—from that house."

16

The Marvelous Story of the Wonder of Wonders
that the Maharal Revealed to the Two Berls Whose
Two Children Were Switched by a Midwife

IN PRAGUE THERE WAS A children's teacher called "Big
Yekl" who engaged two orphan lads from Romania to work
as assistants in his school. Both were named Berl; one, with a
swarthy face, was called "Black Berl," and the other, ruddy-
faced, was called "Red Berl." The two Berls were very fond
of each other and cooperated in every aspect of their lives,
even sharing all their food. They found favor both in the eyes
of the teacher and the townfolk, for they did their work faithfully and honestly. That is why they managed to save up some
money for a dowry and both made fine matches in Prague.

Even after their weddings the two could not part from
each other and they decided to become partners in business.

Their first venture, ritual slaughter in one slaughterhouse, thrived and they gradually prospered. Then they abandoned butchery and began dealing in oxen. Here too they attained such great success they were considered the biggest ox merchants in town and were known as "The Two Rich Berls from Prague." Then they bought a large, walled house in Prague and established their residence together there, living side by side, next door to each other.

Only in the matter of children were the two rich partners unequal, for Red Berl had healthy sons and daughters, alive and well, while Black Berl had no sons but many daughters, not all of whom survived. The wives of both Berls got along amicably and both used the same midwife, known as Estherl the midwife. Still, in her heart of hearts a great envy burned in Black Berl's wife concerning her partner, Red Berl's wife. But since she was wise and of kindly disposition, Black Berl's wife always restrained herself with all her might and displayed no enmity toward Red Berl's wife.

Indeed, Estherl the midwife understood full well what lay in the heart of Black Berl's wife and she was overcome with compassion for her, for she felt the woman's misfortune deep within her. That is why Estherl began to think of plans and schemes how to do Black Berl's wife a big favor. The midwife wanted her to be happy and to enable her to brag to her husband: "Heaven has taken away my disgrace, for I too have given birth to a baby boy."

It so happened the wives of the two Berls went to the ritual bath the same night. When Estherl learned of this, she had the following idea: if both women became pregnant that night and Black Berl's wife had a girl and Red Berl's wife a boy, and if both delivered around the same time, she would secretly switch the babies and place the baby boy next to Black Berl's wife and the baby girl next to Red Berl's wife.

In fact, that is exactly what happened: both became pregnant at the same time and the delivery too took place about the same time. Red Berl's wife went into labor first and gave birth to a boy, but Estherl the midwife cried out, "Mazeltov, it's a girl." She apparently thought that even if Black Berl's wife also had a boy she would switch the babies anyway because Red Berl's children were strong and healthy and more prone to survive than Black Berl's children.

As to her shout of "Mazeltov, it's a girl," she planned to make up an excuse later by saying that since her neighbor, Black Berl's wife, who was longing for a son, was about to give birth, therefore, afraid of the evil eye, she had said a daughter was born until she saw Black Berl's wife's delivery.

The next day the time came for Black Berl's wife to give birth. And what the midwife had hoped for came to pass, for she too gave birth to a boy. The midwife cried out, "Mazeltov!" at the birth of a son and Black Berl's house was full of gladness and joy.

Later, the midwife revealed the truth in Red Berl's house: They too had had a boy and she justified her earlier remark by saying: "To avoid the evil eye and prevent envy, I was afraid of telling the truth until after Black Berl's wife gave birth," an explanation that was accepted in Red Berl's house with cries of approval.

That night, when everyone was asleep in both houses, the midwife secretly switched the babies and no one was aware of her deed. The midwife too kept this matter a deep secret and told no one about it. But in her diary, where she would punctiliously record each day's events, she also described the switch, noting the date, month, and year the two boys were born to the two Berls. She also wrote that she had secretly exchanged the babies and placed the son of Red Berl into the bed of Black Berl's wife and the son of Black Berl in the bed of Red Berl's wife, adding that she did this for a reason known only to herself alone. But since there was no one who would even occasionally glance at her diary, the matter sank into oblivion like a stone cast into deep waters.

The wives of the two Berls nursed their sons and the thought never crossed their minds that they were nursing infants not their own. The boys grew up, each one with parents not his own. Then Estherl the midwife died suddenly and her daughter, a midwife too, inherited her possessions, including Estherl's diary, and brought them to her house. But since the daughter had no need of her mother's diary, she stored it in the cellar along with her other old and unwanted things.

The two Berls began to marry off their children and made excellent matches. However, since Black Berl still had two unmarried daughters and the young son who had been switched, and Red Berl still had four sons, two daughters and the youngest son who also had been switched, the time was not ripe for them to arrange matches with each other.

But for some years now people would often suggest that the two Berls, the loving partners, should also be bound in marriage—that Black Berl's only son marry Red Berl's youngest daughter, who was only one year older than he.

Family and friends all agreed this was a very proper match. In short, they concluded the arrangements, wrote the engagement contract, and prepared a splendid betrothal feast in keeping with the style of the very wealthy.

As the time for the wedding drew near, the two fathers

asked the Maharal to lead the ceremony under the canopy. Such was the custom among prosperous Prague Jews, who tried their utmost to have the great honor of having the Maharal himself officiate at their children's marriage.

The Maharal came to the wedding, but something astounding occurred during the ceremony. When he took the wine goblet to recite the blessing consecrating the marriage, the goblet fell from his hands to the floor and the wine spilled. Everyone assumed that the press of the large crowd had caused the goblet to fall accidentally from the Maharal's hands. Consequently, the guests moved back and made room around the Maharal. The goblet was refilled for the recitation of the blessing.

But nothing helped, for as soon as the Maharal began to chant, "Blessed art Thou," just before he said, "God," the goblet fell to the floor once more. A great fear overwhelmed the Maharal; he was so upset his face turned white. The guests too became frightened and amazed at what had happened.

Meanwhile the old shamesh, Reb Avrohom Chaim, looked at the wine bottle and noticed there was not enough wine to refill the goblet. And since the Maharal's custom was to recite a blessing only over wine from his own cellar, Reb Avrohom Chaim turned to the mute Yossele the golem.

"Run quickly to the Maharal's house," he shouted, "and bring another bottle of wine from the cellar."

Yossele the golem flew from the Great Synagogue where the wedding was taking place to the Maharal's house nearby, but as he approached the door he suddenly stopped in his tracks. From afar it looked as if he was talking and arguing with someone unseen.

Many in the wedding party yelled, "Bring the wine!" to him, but rather than going to the cellar, Yossele the golem went to the courtroom where he wrote a little note composed of eight words: "The groom and bride are brother and sister."

So instead of wine Yossele the golem brought the note to the wedding canopy and handed it to the Maharal. The enraged guests wanted to tear Yossele the golem apart like a herring. But they realized at once that he was not someone to fool with. Everyone fell silent, waiting to see what would happen next.

Seeing the note agitated the Maharal even more and his face turned red.

"Ah, woe!" he cried out. "Brother and sister!"

The guests were stunned at this astonishing turn of events and gathered that something strange had taken place. Meanwhile they all heard the Maharal asking Yossele the golem: "Who told you the groom and bride are brother and sister?"

Yossele the golem moved a few steps away from the crush of the crowd and gestured to the Maharal to follow him. He pointed to a window of the synagogue to indicate that the man still standing there had revealed the secret to him and ordered him to inform the Maharal too. The Maharal followed and stood facing the window. He looked up and gazed at it for a while as did all the people—but they saw nothing. Then the Maharal rejoined the guests.

"The ceremony can no longer take place today," he announced as he stood again under the canopy, "because a thorough investigation will first have to be initiated . . ." And then he gave the order, "Distribute the wedding feast food among the poor."

That night, after midnight, the Maharal summoned Yossele the golem privately to his room, gave him a secret order, and handed him his staff. Yossele the golem then ran to a point outside the city, came back an hour later to the Maharal, and returned his staff. Later it was learned that the golem had gone to the cemetery by order of the rabbi to summon the dead Estherl the midwife to prepare herself for the courtroom trial the following day before the Maharal.

The next morning the Maharal ordered: "Set a place for me and the two other judges in the Great Synagogue a few feet from the northeast corner and put up a small wooden partition. Then proclaim that no one who prays here this morning should go home after services but remain in the synagogue and stand on the western side behind the bimah."

After the Maharal had finished praying, he sat at the prepared table with the two other judges, all of them wrapped in their tallis and tefillin. Then the rabbi sent the old shamesh, Reb Avrohom Chaim, to bring the in-laws—the two Berls and their wives—and also the groom and the bride. When they arrived in the synagogue, the rabbi placed them at the southern side of the table. He asked the two Berls and their wives to tell him everything they had said and done after their weddings. From their remarks he concluded that they had not deliberately exchanged the babies or consented to the switch.

Then the Maharal called Yossele the golem and placed his staff in his hand. In the presence of the entire congregation he commanded him: "Yossele, please go to the cemetery and bring back to us the soul of Estherl the midwife so that she can give us a full explanation."

The Maharal also handed Yossele the golem a little note and he left the synagogue. All the men in the synagogue, now terror-stricken, began whispering to one another. Then the Maharal stood and called out loudly to them: "I am asking you not to be afraid. Remain calm, for no harm will befall you."

The entire congregation fell silent and calmed down. Half an hour later Yossele the golem approached the Maharal and returned his staff. He also pointed to the wooden barrier erected in the corner of the synagogue and signaled that he had fulfilled his mission—the woman was now behind the partition.

A pall of death fell upon everyone. The entire congregation seemed to be petrified; they closed their eyes and did not budge. Then the Maharal's voice was heard, speaking loudly to the dead woman.

"We, the court of the lower realm, decree that you, Esther, tell us down to the last detail how it came about that this groom and bride are brother and sister."

The dead woman immediately began to tell the story from beginning to end of how she had switched the baby boys and why she had done this.

"I acted not out of treachery or nastiness but out of compassion and for the sake of peace between the two Berls' wives."

The men gathered in the synagogue heard only the sound of the midwife's voice, but the judges, the in-laws, and the groom and bride heard everything and understood every word Estherl said.

At the end of her remarks the dead woman added, "It is now twelve years after my death and my soul still has not found proper repose and will not find it until I set aright what I have ruined. And because of the merit of the Maharal I was granted permission to prevent him from officiating at the wedding ceremony of a brother and sister due to my switching the babies. Because had the ceremony not been interrupted my soul would have been swallowed up into the lowest depths of hell without any chance of redemption."

The midwife concluded her remarks amid weeping.

"Have pity on my soul and set the matter right," she asked the court. "Return each of the sons to his rightful family and ask the in-laws and the groom and bride to forgive me with all their heart. And then my soul will be bound up in the bond of everlasting life."

Then Estherl said further, "If the court does not believe me, I can offer proof about my statements. Look for my diary, which is an account of the babies whose midwife I have been, and you will see recorded there the day, month, and year the children were born. The fact that I switched the babies for a reason known only to me is also recorded there. And had I been of sound mind at the time of my death, I surely would have confessed this deed and been scrupulous about setting the matter right. But because I died suddenly and my rational faculty also ceased at once I couldn't correct this wrong in time before my death."

Now her words could no longer be heard—only the sound of weeping. And the entire congregation in the synagogue wept along with her.

Hearing that this entire story was written in her diary, the Maharal immediately sent his two shamoshim to summon the midwife's daughter to appear before him and bring all the diaries written by her dead mother.

The men tarried there a full hour until they found the half-torn diary in the cellar. They brought it to the Maharal and found that everything the dead Estherl had said was true.

The Maharal and his two judges began discussing the verdict to be rendered. First they decided that the dead Estherl the midwife had to request forgiveness from the groom and bride who had been humiliated because of her. And if the two offered her a complete pardon she would be considered innocent and free of all punishment.

At once the tearful voice of the dead woman was heard saying: "I, Estherl, who was your midwife, hereby request your forgiveness."

"We forgive you completely," the groom and bride replied.

Then the Maharal and his two judges stood and declared aloud: "We, of the court of the lower realm, exempt you, Estherl the midwife, from all punishment. You will also be exempt from all punishment in the upper realm. Go in peace and rest in peace until final peace comes."

Then the Maharal gave the order: "Take the dividing partition that was put in the corner of the synagogue and push it aside as a sign that the dead woman is no longer here."

Now the Maharal called all the men who had gathered in the synagogue and told them: "We now know the truth of the incident concerning the exchange of the two Berls' babies by Estherl the midwife. Therefore, this groom and bride should be considered brother and sister, children of Red Berl. And moreover, the youngest son of Red Berl is really Black Berl's only son."

The Maharal further suggested: "It seems to me that if the two Berls and their children are willing, it would be just if they remained in-laws as before—Black Berl's only son should marry the bride, Red Berl's youngest daughter, and the wedding should take place quickly, in fact, next week."

The two Berls immediately consented to the Maharal's proposal. They asked their children, who also agreed. The Maharal ordered the new engagement contract written then and there in the synagogue in the presence of the entire congregation. This was done. Wine and cakes were distributed to everyone and the Maharal gave them his blessings.

Then the Maharal ordered the synagogue's great book of records brought to him. He inscribed a summary of this incident in the book and signed his name. He also told the judges to sign their names too. The Maharal blessed the groom and bride with good fortune and success in their match and then sent everyone home. He also ordered: "Take a plank from the partition placed in the corner in front of the dead woman and nail it in as a permanent memorial." The shamoshim did this.

The wedding took place the following week amid great splendor. The Maharal himself officiated and also attended the wedding feast. He was very happy that Heaven had prevented him from marrying a brother and sister. This match lasted many years in Prague. The couple contributed generously to charity and they lived a pleasant life of wealth and honor.

17

The Astounding Story of the Torah
That Fell to the Floor on Yom Kippur

IN PRAGUE, IN 1587, A SAD incident occurred on Yom Kippur after the Mincha Torah reading in the Great Synagogue, where the Maharal prayed. One of the congregants, who was honored with the mitzva of lifting up the Torah, let it slip from his hands and the Torah fell to the floor. This sorely grieved and depressed the Maharal.

First, he ordained that everyone who had witnessed the Torah falling was to fast on the day prior to the Eve of Sukkos. However, the Maharal understood that his moral obligation would not be fulfilled with such fasting, for the Rock of Israel does not desire fasts but the extirpation of the evil deeds that prompted the above incident. For surely the Torah falling was not a gratuitous event.

Although the Maharal diligently investigated the cause of

this incident, he was not successful and felt sad of heart. On the day of the fast, during a dream, the Maharal asked heaven to inform him why the Torah had fallen. But he was not given a clear answer, merely a hint, like an unresolved riddle whose solution the Maharal could not fathom.

The reply was a jumble of words and letters the Maharal could not understand: "Do not wyw lien kym tr."

The Maharal then decided to use Yossele the golem for this matter too, and he came up with the following idea. He wrote the seventeen letters of all the words on seventeen pieces of paper, each letter on a different piece, and he mixed them up. Then he summoned Yossele the golem and told him: "Line up all the letters in one row so that one letter joins another for easy reading and comprehension."

Yossele the golem did not ask or probe, neither did he delve deeply. He merely set the pieces of paper in the following order: "Do not lie wynw yk m tr."

The Maharal saw at once that it meant: "Do not lie *w*ith *y*our *n*eighbor's *w*ife to defile yourself with her. *Y*om *K*ippur *M*incha *T*orah *r*eading."

The Maharal quickly realized that this quotation from the Yom Kippur Mincha Torah reading hinted that the man who had been given the honor of lifting up the Torah had transgressed with a married woman. He sent Yossele the golem to that man with a letter summoning the man under suspicion immediately to the Maharal. And when Yossele the golem was sent to summon someone, that man knew it was absolutely forbidden to refuse or even delay and temporarily postpone the matter. For it had happened more than once that Yossele the golem would snatch the reluctant man, put him on his shoulder, and carry him through the streets of the city to the Maharal's house, like one carries a sheep to slaughter.

The man under suspicion, the one who had lifted the Torah, came at once to the Maharal, who brought him into a private chamber and locked the door. "I'm asking you to admit in good faith the sin you've committed," the Maharal told him, "for the Torah fell to the floor on Yom Kippur only because of your sin."

The man realized he had been caught by the Maharal like a fish on a hook and knew he could not deny his wrongdoing. So he immediately confessed his misdeed and declared: "I have been sinning for a long time with my partner's wife."

The Maharal imposed a certain penance on the man and also sent for the sinning woman, and the matter was set aright according to the law.

18

The Attack on Yossele the Golem

DURING THE MAHARAL'S TENURE as Chief Rabbi of Prague, whenever Jews quarreled they had the despicable custom—habitual with them—of insulting and denigrating one another with the epithet "nadler." This term was uglier and far worse than "bastard," for "nadler" suggested that pure Jewish blood did not flow in that person's veins. This insult had taken root among them during the Expulsion from Spain and Italy, when many Jews were forced to apostatize and pass into the gentile community. After the decree of Expulsion was annulled these Jews returned to their faith in other lands.

Many of these Conversos also came to Prague and many had wives from other countries who later converted to Judaism. The barbs of the insulting appellation "nadler" were aimed at their children and their descendants.

When the Maharal saw that this caused havoc in the lives

of some families and even affected some of the leading Torah luminaries of the generation, he was determined to eradicate this ugly curse from Jewish lips so that no one in Prague or the rest of the country would ever utter that word again.

The Maharal assembled many great rabbis and gaons from all over the country and, to the accompaniment of ram's horn sounds and black candles, they promulgated a severe and awesome ban of excommunication on anyone who let the demeaning word "nadler" pass his lips to offend a fellow Jew, no matter who he was. The Maharal's ban had its desired effect and the Jews took great care not to use this humiliating term.

However, no cities are devoid of base and impudent men. Among the circle of porters in Prague, three arrogant, licentious, and insolent scoundrels were still using the offensive insult, "nadler," several weeks after the promulgated ban. Hearing this, the Maharal was furious. He sent the old shamesh, Reb Avrohom Chaim, to summon the leader of these hooligans. The Maharal planned to persuade him in a peaceable manner to desist from this evil path. But the porter paid no attention to the shamesh's remarks and refused to go with him. "I'm too busy now," he declared, laughing at the shamesh. "I'll go when I have some time."

When the shamesh related to the Maharal the porter's

brazen response, the rabbi became even more incensed. He assembled a few sturdy youths and told them to prepare a batch of switches and some strong rope. Then he summoned Yossele the golem and told him: "Go seize that porter now, throw him over your shoulder, and bring him to the courtroom."

Yossele the golem departed at once for the porter's house. He sought and found him, grabbed him by the scruff of his neck, and threw him over his shoulder. Then he carried him like a sheep through the streets of the city and brought him to the courtroom. Even though this porter was no weakling either and always bullied everyone, against Yossele the golem his bravado vanished, and after Yossele the golem graced him with a few smacks he had to submit to him.

Once the Maharal was informed of the porter's presence in the court, he ordered: "Bind him with the rope and lash him with the switches as much as he can bear so he'll remember for a long time the honor accorded to him. Now he'll think twice before uttering that despicable word again."

The Maharal's command was carried out by those young men along with Yossele the golem, who stood next to the porter and went at it vigorously like an ox driver goading his ox. After the beating, the men ordered the porter: "Take off your sandals and go barefoot to the Maharal for a rebuke. Once you admit your wrong and promise you won't commit any further folly, the Maharal will lift the ban that's been placed on you."

The porter was obliged to obey all the orders. Afterward, he plucked up his remaining strength and sluggishly made his way home as though crawling on all fours.

At home he had to lie in bed about two weeks until his wounds healed and he recuperated sufficiently to walk normally again. But in the scourged porter's heart the fire of revenge burned secretly and he decided to get even with the men who had whipped him. Most of all he wanted revenge against Yossele the golem. He not only sought bruise for bruise literally, but desired to totally eliminate the golem from this world.

The porter secretly summoned his friends and told them: "Let's deal shrewdly with Yossele the golem and come up with a scheme to finally get rid of him."

They decided to take him by surprise and could easily have killed him had he been someone else and not Yossele the golem. This is the plan they devised. It was the Maharal's custom to have fresh water brought to him from a deep well on Saturday night which was heated up for his enjoyment.

Before the arrival of Yossele the golem, the other shamoshim would bring the rabbi the pitcher of water. But because it was often bitterly cold in winter and the ground near the well was ice-covered, they slipped several times and fell with the pitcher of water. Therefore, using Yossele the golem for such errands was a great boon in such instances and he was given the task of taking the pitcher and drawing water from the well every Saturday night after Havdala.

He never slacked off and was not fazed by cold or snow or darkness of night. He did not even wait for the order but went on his own to bring the water.

And that is how the attack on Yossele the golem was planned. On Saturday night during Hanuka, when it was freezing cold and icy, the hooligans hid by that well. Yossele the golem approached and lowered the pole with the bucket into the well to draw water. When he bent his head and, as drawers of water are wont to do, lowered most of his torso into the space of the well, his hidden attackers struck.

They seized Yossele the golem's legs and threw him into the well, head first and legs up. Before the golem could twist out of their hands he was already cast into the water. The pole and the empty bucket went flying out of the well and Yossele the golem got thoroughly soaked as he sank into the depths of the well. Then he floated up and began flailing the water with his hands. Knowing that this would be his end, the hooligans had prepared heavy stones in advance which they now threw into the well to smash Yossele the golem's skull and force him to drown.

And so it happened. The stones rained down on his head and injured his nose and one eye, making him sink deeper into the water. As soon as the hooligans had thrown all the stones down at him they fled. But Yossele the golem saved himself by floating up again.

Meanwhile, the men at the Maharal's house waited for the water to prepare the hot drink for the rabbi. Seeing that Yossele the golem had not returned with the pitcher of water, the old shamesh, Reb Avrohom Chaim, took a lamp, called two other men, and went to the well to look for the golem.

On the ground near the well they recognized the Maharal's pitcher and realized at once that something was amiss. They shone the lamp into the well to look for Yossele the golem. As soon as he saw the light the golem began splashing to signal his presence.

Then the men lowered the pole with the bucket in which Yossele the golem sat until they pulled him out of the well, barely alive, bruised, wounded, and bloodied. They took him back to the Maharal's house, where they removed his wet clothes, bathed his wounds, and bandaged his head.

The Maharal immediately came to see Yossele the golem. "You will be fine," he assured him and instructed the men, "Lay him down in his bed next to the stove."

There Yossele the golem warmed himself and fell asleep. But it was not until three days later that he was able to leave his bed to go outside, walking with a cane. On that day the Maharal summoned him: "What happened to you by the well?" he asked. "And do you know who did this to you?"

Yossele the golem answered by writing down everything that had happened to him. He also told the Maharal that among the attackers he recognized the porter who had been whipped in the courtroom. In noting this, Yossele also asked the Maharal for permission to have his revenge of the porter.

"No, I will not let you do this," the Maharal replied, "for retribution will come suddenly from heaven."

Soon thereafter a black mange suddenly infested the porter's arm, an extremely dangerous excrescence called "the black scurf." To prevent the infection from spreading on his body, the doctors cut pieces of his flesh daily, but since nothing helped they concluded there was no hope for him.

Then the porter acknowledged that he was punished only because of his disrespect for the Maharal. He narrated down to the minutest detail how he and three of his friends had attacked Yossele the golem, thrown him into the well, and rained large stones down on him. The porter then sent his wife and sons to the Maharal to weep before him, beg for his forgiveness, and request that he remove the plague of death from him.

But the Maharal refused to see them and the porter died an excruciating death. Thereafter, his three friends who had helped him attack the golem visited the Maharal and tearfully confessed their wrongdoing, for they feared they might die like the porter. They justified their behavior by saying, "The porter enticed us and even bribed us to join him, but now we regret our deed . . . We're asking for forgiveness, and we'll take upon ourselves any penance and pay any fines you impose on us."

The Maharal ordered them to pay a certain sum to the yeshiva to support Torah study. "As for penance, each of you will have to fast forty days this year and each week recite the entire Book of Psalms."

The porters did this and by obeying all of the Maharal's instructions they remained alive.

19

An Awesome Tale About the Ruin near Prague

NEAR PRAGUE, CLOSE TO THE ROAD that leads into the city, stood an old ruin. In former times this building had been a gunpowder factory. On account of its location near the road, the authorities had to be careful of passersby. Moreover, because it was old and full of cracks and breaches, the government did not want to repair the building. Instead, they moved the factory further away from the city, to a building between the army barracks and the king's castle.

Owing to this neglect, the building became more and more dilapidated and it remained a ruin for a long time. Meanwhile, it became defiled and demons danced there. The ruin now cast a pall of fear and terror on everyone who passed it at night. Many people averred that at night they heard something that sounded like a chorus singing. Others claimed that at night they saw a pack of hundreds of black dogs roving around the ruin. Another Jew swore that one night, as he walked by, he saw a soldier standing on the roof playing a big flute like the one used by the army to call soldiers to muster.

All these stories prompted passersby to carefully avoid the narrow lane next to the ruin at night and walk only on the other side.

Once, a Jewish merchant from Prague who sold goods to the country folk returned home from a village. Setting caution aside, he walked along the narrow path near the ruin from whence a black dog ran toward him, barking. The dog circled him and then bounded back to the ruin. The terror-stricken merchant returned home, weak in the knees, his hair bristling in fear. After telling his family about his encounter with the demonic pest he lay down to sleep.

During the night, however, the man began barking like a dog in his sleep and his frightened family quickly woke him. In so doing, they noticed he was drenched in sweat and lay there thoroughly drained and exhausted.

"I dreamed I was riding on a black dog," he told them, "along with many other men who like me were riding in one row in an orderly manner just like soldiers. When all the riders began barking like dogs, I too was forced to bark. For I had been warned that if I refused to bark the dogs would de-

vour me alive then and there. And that's why I too had to bark
with all my might."

The members of his family pooh-poohed the dream and
tried to convince him that it was no cause for alarm. "It's only
your thoughts before falling asleep that prompted a dream
like this. If you stopped thinking such thoughts during the
day," they suggested, "you would have a restful sleep."

But in the middle of the next night the merchant resumed
his barking of the previous night. And so it continued from
one night to the next until he became feeble and no longer
had the strength to walk. His flesh grew lean and he became
impoverished for he had become too frail to provide for his
family who were now weak with hunger.

When the family realized the extent of their misfortune,
the merchant gathered his last reserve of strength and went
with his wife and little children to the Maharal's house.
They came to him weeping profusely. "Save us, please!"
they cried.

The merchant told the Maharal tearfully everything that
had happened to him. "My children are dependent on me,"
he said, "and I can't earn a living. My little ones are asking for
bread and there is none."

"Inspect the man's ritual fringes," was the first thing the

Maharal ordered, "to see if they are kosher." One fringe was found defective.

Then the Maharal bade, "Examine the man's telfillin."

His hand telfillin was also found to have a flaw.

"That's why the merchant doesn't have divine protection," the Maharal declared, "and that's why he has fallen into mud and filth, which is unclean, because it is written, 'For He will order His angels to guard you wherever you go.' This means that two angels accompany every Jew to protect him from evil occurrences. And these angels are created from the two mitzvas of ritual fringes and tefillin. One can see that his is so for according to *gematria,* the sum of the letters of the above verse equals the sum of the letters of ritual fringes and two tefillin." That is why the Maharal told the merchant, "First repair your ritual fringes and your tefillin to make them kosher and then immerse yourself in the ritual bath."

Then the Maharal called his scribe and told him to write on kosher parchment the following amulet:

No dog shall bark at any of the Israelites.

Dog no bark	Bark no dog
No bark dog	Dog bark no
Bark dog no	No dog bark.

"Before you go to sleep at night," the Maharal decreed, "tie this amulet to your forehead, with the writing facing outward." He also told the merchant: "Do not sleep at home for the next seven nights but go to the courtroom and sleep in Yossele the golem's bed." And then the rabbi turned to Yossele the golem. "And for those seven nights you will sleep in the merchant's bed."

Everyone obeyed the Maharal's orders. The ailing man slept well in Yossele the golem's bed and felt no more of that evil affliction.

After midnight on the seventh night, the Maharal summoned Yossele the golem. He placed his staff in his hands and gave him a tinderbox. "Take also the two big bundles of straw we've prepared and bring them into the ruin," the Maharal ordered. "Ignite the straw near the roof so that the entire ruin goes up in flames."

The golem carried out all the Maharal's instructions and the entire ruin was set ablaze.

From that time on the ruin never caused any more problems. On the seventh day the Maharal took the amulet from the man and told him: "Now return home to sleep as before."

The man's sleep was sweet, his strength returned, and he was as vigorous and healthy as in former times.

20

A Wondrous Tale About Duke Bartholomew

A VERY WEALTHY DUKE ONCE LIVED in a big beautiful village several kilometers east of Prague. He owned ten villages and many fields and forests. The duke's village had a spacious park where one could meditate and in whose midst stood a small palace with a high tower topped with a short spire. Surrounding the palace was a thick wall and a deep, magnificent moat over which, at one point, hung an iron drawbridge suspended by thick chains. This palace was absolutely empty. Nothing was in it. But in the middle of it two long marble headstones lay side by side above what were obviously two graves. Two names were engraved on the marble; on one stone the name of the mother; on the other, the name of the son.

There is a wonderful story about this mother and this son.

In former times an old duke named Bartholomew who liked Jews lived in that village. His sole offspring was an only son, born late in his life. In his ten villages lived many Jews, who managed all of the duke's business affairs, which provided them with an excellent livelihood. After the duke became a widower, in order to forget his sorrow he had the custom of visiting the Jewish villagers' homes with his son. He was especially fond of greeting his Jews on Sabbaths and holidays. At one Jew's house he would eat fish; at a second, potato pudding, and so on.

In the duke's village lived a rich Jewish leaseholder named Moshe who had a beautiful and intelligent daughter the same age as the duke's son. The duke's son found the leaseholder's daughter attractive and he always liked to talk to her.

Once, when the old duke and his son were visiting the leaseholder on a Sabbath, eating fish and drinking wine, the old duke said to the Jewish farmer: "Moshke, I want you to know, if your daughter would consent to convert, my son would marry her. And for her sake you too will benefit from this, for I will cancel your leaseholder's rental fee."

The duke's words cut the leaseholder to the quick. But wisely he made naught of the duke's remarks and replied with a faint smile: "It would not be a fitting match for your son nor a good bargain for him—for he can easily get a beautiful, rich, and educated girl who also stems from a distinguished ducal family."

"In my eyes." the duke replied with a laugh, "the Jewish lineage is more distinguished than that of a duke."

They spoke no more of this matter. But the leaseholder knew that the duke's remark was not mere empty talk, for as the proverb has it: When wine goes in, secrets go out. The leaseholder feared that his daughter might be destined to fall into the hands of the duke's son. He therefore hurriedly arranged a match for her and she was engaged to an excellent Torah scholar, an orphan from a fine Prague family. And soon the wedding was celebrated in all its splendor.

A year after the wedding a son was born to this couple and they all ate at the table of their father, Moshe the leaseholder. One year later the plague spread through the land. Entire families succumbed so quickly there were not enough gravediggers to bury them immediately. And many families fled to other lands, not knowing who was alive and who had died. In short, the villagers ran to wherever their legs carried them and many did not know where their friends had gone.

The epidemic did not spare the duke's villages either. Moshe the leaseholder and his wife died. Some of his children living in the village died too, and some fled to another country. The son-in-law he had brought from Prague also died, leaving only the leaseholder's young daughter with her baby boy. Since the gravediggers did not come quickly enough to bury her family, she could no longer remain in the house with the dead and she too fled with her son. Not knowing where to turn, she entered the duke's park to seek some repose from her misery. When the old duke and his only son learned of this, they pitied her and her baby boy. They gave her a separate house in the duke's courtyard and provided her with everything she needed.

In Prague, and in all the duke's villages as well, people assumed that the leaseholder's entire family had perished. In time, the leaseholder's daughter forgot her misfortune and began to adorn herself to look attractive in the way she had during her youth. The duke's only son gradually began to draw closer to her until soon they were so bound with the bonds of love that they decided to bind themselves in marriage. To conceal the fact that she was the leaseholder's daughter, she and her little son were secretly sent to Venice. After a wet nurse was engaged there for the baby boy the wedding was soon celebrated in that city.

The old duke spread the word in his village that his only son had married the daughter of the king's councilor in Venice and that they would come back in a year. During this time all went well with the newly married pair. They traveled to many lands as was the custom among dukes. Only after a year and a half did the new couple return to the village amid great honor. No one even dreamed that the young duke's wife was Jewish, the daughter of Moshke the leaseholder, for with no one left of his family his name had already been forgotten in the village. They also let it be known that she had given birth to a boy in Venice, who was now being tended by a wet nurse and would be brought back to his parents in the village after he was weaned.

Not long thereafter the old duke died and all his wealth, all his lands, and his ducal title were inherited by his only son.

Half a year later, after he had been weaned, the baby boy was brought to the village. Since his Hebrew name was Yaakov, he was listed in the village birth registry as Yaakov Bartholomew, the son born to the young duke. The young duke loved his Jewish wife very much and they lived happily. In the village, she gave birth to two beautiful girls. This young duke also loved the Jews who dwelled in his villages. He let them manage all his businesses and followed in his father's footsteps. But in one matter he did ill, and this is what he did.

Because the young duke knew the truth—that his little boy was of Jewish stock and that because everything seeks its roots, he feared the boy might convert and ruin his entire estate. Therefore, he came up with the idea of attempting to plant the poison of anti-Semitism in Yaakov's heart. He engaged tutors whom he knew were vehement anti-Semites and ordered them to teach the boy to despise the People of Israel. In so doing, the teachers rooted in the boy's heart a hatred of Jews that kept increasing as time went by—to the point where he scrupulously avoided even speaking to a Jew.

The young duke's three children grew in beauty and learning. His wife's son, Yaakov Bartholomew, married the daughter of an army officer, and his two daughters were married in other countries and left their father's house for their husbands' homelands. Now the only people in the duke's house were Yaakov Bartholomew and his wife.

Years passed. The duke died at the age of sixty and his wife, the Jewish daughter of the leaseholder, was left a widow. She now lived with her son, Yaakov, who inherited all the wealth, all the villages, and the ducal title as well.

The young duke began to rule over all ten villages—but this created a new misfortune. Since he had had only anti-Semitic tutors and had been accustomed from his youth to anti-Jewish teachings, a great hatred for Jews remained in his heart. And so he began to oppress them and make all the Jews who lived in the ten villages miserable. Little by little he deprived them of their livelihood. At first he burdened the Jews with extra taxes; then he decided to expel them from the villages altogether and let others manage all his business affairs.

According to this decree of banishment, about one hundred Jewish families would have had to pick up the wanderer's staff and seek livelihood elsewhere. With the unfortunate time drawing near, the Jews got together and decided to go to Prague and seek the Maharal's counsel about the impending calamity. They met the Maharal and, amid tears, poured out their bitter hearts to him. "Have pity on us and on our families," they begged him. "Save us so that we can stay in our homes and maintain our livelihood."

But the Maharal replied, "I have no advice for you now. Nevertheless, I have hope and confidence that Heaven will very likely inspire me with a plan how to save you. . . . Now return to your homes and pray to our God in Heaven. Don't tell anyone you came to ask me for help—but come back to see me in a week."

That night the father of the new duke appeared from the Upper World in the Maharal's dream. In it the dead man bitterly told the Maharal the entire story: "The new duke, Yaakov Bartholomew, is a Jew whom I—a Jew named Yitzchok ben Aharon Halevi from Prague—have fathered. I was the son-in-law of Reb Moshe the leaseholder who had lived in the duke's village. He and I died in the epidemic, leaving my wife, Roise, Moshe the leaseholder's daughter, a widow with a baby boy. The duke who died married her and then, lying to everyone, claimed Roise's baby, Yaakov, as his own. He told everyone that Yaakov was their son—but the truth is, he is my son.

"From the moment my son, Yaakov Bartholomew, took over governing all the villages and began to oppress and tyrannize all the Jews who lived in his villages and deny them the opportunity of making a living by the decree of expulsion from all his villages," the dead man complained woefully, "their prayers and tears have ascended to heaven. That's why I feel so terribly tormented in the Upper World, where I suffer embarrassment, humiliation, and persecution. They give me no peace there and have now driven me back to this world to set aright what my son has done.

"I have appeared several times to my son in a dream," the dead man continued telling the Maharal, "and informed him that he is a Jew by birth and that his mother is a Jew. To accent the truth of my statement, I explained that he can see for himself that he was circumcised. In the dream I asked him to leave the poor Jews alone and let them stay in their homes. But does he pay attention to dreams? That is why I am earnestly requesting you in this dream to have pity on my soul and to formulate a wise and intelligent plan to make the duke, my son, cancel his evil scheme. . . . And please don't say you don't have the power to save the community—for I have heard in the True World," the dead man concluded, telling the Maharal, "that only you with your extraordinary wisdom can accomplish this salvation."

The next day the Maharal told the old shamesh, Reb Avrohom Chaim: "I want you to thoroughly investigate the truth of the assertion that a Jewish leaseholder named Moshe with a daughter named Roise had once lived in the duke's village and that in Prague at that time a young man named Yitzchok ben Aharon Halevi became that leaseholder's son-in-law."

Reb Avrohom Chaim researched the municipal records and also inquired of the elders. He ascertained that indeed it was all true and correct. And when the old shamesh reported this to the Maharal, the rabbi declared: "Now that we have verified the words of the dead man whom I saw in my dream, what he heard in the True World about me saving them is also surely true. And if so, we have to come up with a plan how to save them."

And this was the Maharal's wonderful idea. After learning that Duke Bartholomew attended services in the cloister in Prague every Sunday, the Maharal wrote the following letter in the local language:

My dear son,

I have come from the Upper World to inform you that I, Yitzchok ben Aharon Halevi from Prague, am your real father. I was the first husband of your mother, Roise, who lives with you. She is the daughter of a Jew, Moshe the leaseholder, who once lived in your village during the old duke's reign.

I and my father-in-law Moshe died during the epidemic. And it was I who named you Yaakov. And now I have come to ask you not to harm the Jews who have dwelled among you in the villages from time immemorial.

I have already told you this several times in dreams. But seeing that you pay no heed to dreams, I was obliged to come down to you from the Upper World myself and hand you this letter pertaining to this matter, because ever since the tears of these oppressed families have risen up to heaven I have no repose—only bitter and severe torments.

And whether you realize the truth of this from the fact that you are circumcised like all other Jews, or whether you ask your mother and tell her what happened to you during your trip and show her this letter, you will no longer be able to deny this but will be forced to admit that all this is indeed true.

I also want you to know, my son, that if you need advice on any matter, consult the rabbi of the Jews of Prague. Do whatever he tells you and you will succeed.

Your father,
Yitzchok ben Aharon Halevi

This was the text of the letter. And on the day Duke Yaakov Bartholomew had planned to come to the cloister in Prague, the Maharal summoned Yossele the golem in the morning and handed him the letter. He also gave him the famous amulet that made him invisible.

On the road to Prague, near the city—the route that the duke took—was a little hill where all the wagons slowed down. "Go to that hill," the Maharal told Yossele the golem, "and wait there with the letter until the duke's covered wagon drawn by four horses starts climbing the hill. Then approach his wagon, put the letter on the duke's lap, move away calmly, and come back home."

Yossele the golem followed all of the Maharal's instructions. When the duke suddenly saw the letter on his lap he became very frightened. He turned this way and that but saw no one. He opened the letter and realized that no one but his dead father could have sent it and a pall of terror came over him.

Returning to his home, the duke questioned his mother thoroughly about this matter and showed her the letter. She too was very astounded and scared. "All of this is true," she admitted, "and it is not right to persecute these Jewish families, for they are our brothers and sisters."

"If so, what will become of us?" Duke Yaakov Bartholomew asked his mother, completely bewildered. "I was born a Jew and made a Christian without my knowledge. Now I don't know to which camp I belong."

The next day the duke sent his covered wagon to the Maharal with a letter requesting that he come to his house. At once the Maharal knew the reason for the invitation and gave an order to inform all the Jews of the villages that their salvation had come.

The Maharal visited the duke and spent an entire day and

night there, but what he spoke of he did not wish to reveal. Only this was known to all—that the Duke Yaakov Bartholomew gave the Maharal a vast sum of money for a good cause. The Maharal used the money to establish a big yeshiva in Prague and immediately named it the Beis Yaakov Yeshiva, in honor of its founder, Duke Yaakov Bartholomew.

As for the Jewish families who lived in his villages, obviously they were not expelled—on the contrary, the duke greatly reduced their rents. And from that time forward he greeted every Jew cordially with a cheerful countenance.

Some years later, Duke Yaakov Bartholomew built his famous palace in the middle of his park and beautified it with all kinds of adornments. He prepared two graves there, one for his mother and one for himself so that after their deaths they would not have to be buried in the Christian cemetery, for they obviously could not be buried in the Jewish cemetery either. With no other choice, they had to be buried in a separate grave in the park.

21

The Last Blood Libel in Prague During the Maharal's Lifetime

THREE YEARS PASSED IN PEACE and, thanks to the Maharal, neither Prague nor the rest of the country experienced any blood libel tragedy—for the enemies of Israel trembled with fear upon hearing of the wondrous deeds of the Maharal who, by virtue of his great wisdom, was able to uncover all mysteries.

Nevertheless, in 1589 another terrible blood libel took place in Prague. Here is what happened:

A very rich man of a good family named Reb Aharon Gins lived in Prague. He was both learned and prosperous. In him Torah learning and eminence were combined. He had three married daughters and supported his three scholarly sons-in-law, who continuously studied Torah. He also had three sons and another daughter, none of whom was married. Reb

Aharon's business was tanning hides. He lived with his family in a walled house in the city, and his tannery—with twenty full-time employees, twelve Jews and eight Christians—was located in a suburb.

After these tanners had worked together for some years the Christians learned to speak Yiddish just like Jews. Among the Christian workers were three brothers from a village four kilometers from Prague. They had no father, only a poor, elderly mother who lived in an earthen house at the edge of the village. The two older brothers were called Karl Kozlovski and Heinrich Kozlovski, but the name of the much younger third brother was not known in the tannery. He was nicknamed "Kozilek" because he started working in the tannery while still quite young and was a wild boy who loved to dance and prance like an imp.

Ashamed of his real name, the two older brothers never wanted to reveal it. The authorities did not permit his father's family name to be recorded in the municipal birth registry, for his unmarried mother, Jadvina, had borne him two years after becoming a widow. Therefore, he was recorded in the birth registry as a bastard with only his mother's name. His real name was Jan.

The two older brothers, already married with children,

were living in Prague. And since their widowed mother was a poor washerwoman who could neither care for nor properly support her son, she pleaded with her two older sons, "Ask the tannery owner to hire your young brother and this way he'll constantly be under your watchful eye."

The brothers acceded to her request and kept asking Reb Aharon Gins about a job for Kozilek until he finally consented. When the boy started working at the tannery he was fifteen years old. After three years of diligent labor, he began receiving the wages of a full-fledged employee. During that period an incident occurred that stemmed from his uninhibited frolicking, habitual with him since childhood. While jumping from one spot to another he fell into a pit of stinking liquid in which untanned hides had been soaking. He was pulled out, injured and in pain, just barely alive, then lay in his sickbed, ailing for two weeks.

Surgeons also operated on his right hand and amputated two fingers. Gradually, Kozilek recuperated, but now he was no longer capable of doing his former tasks. For besides his maimed right hand with its missing two fingers, he had become physically debilitated and walked about in a state of perpetual fatigue, sometimes even spitting up blood.

Reb Aharon Gins wanted to dismiss Kozilek because he

was not doing his assigned job at the tannery and he did not want to pay wages in vain. But Kozilek's two brothers stood up firmly to the tannery owner and did not let him be ill-treated. They adamantly demanded that Kozilek keep his job and get his former wages. "And if you insist on firing him," they told the owner, "we demand that you pay Kozilek a large sum of money for becoming crippled at your tannery."

This disagreement between the brothers and Reb Aharon Gins prompted several arguments. Eventually, however, they compromised. Kozilek would stay on but work as a porter and sweep up the trash in the tannery and the courtyard. As for wages, they agreed he would get only half his former pay.

From then on the fire of revenge against Reb Aharon Gins smoldered secretly in the brothers' hearts and they schemed vengeance, since they considered the compromise a terrible injustice—and Kozilek's work, carrying everything and gathering the garbage, humiliating hard labor. In addition to his job in the tannery, he had to go to Reb Aharon's house in Prague, clean the yard, and heat up the stoves on Sabbath.

Kozilek always cried in front of his brothers and bemoaned his bitter fate, for the doctors told him that tuberculosis had penetrated his body and he constantly spat up more blood. He was disgusted with his life and felt he had no recourse but to abandon his job and flee while he still had living breath in him. Perhaps he would be cured once he was free.

On Purim day, toward evening, after the table had been set in his house, Reb Aharon Gins sat down with his entire family for the Purim feast. And because most people love the rich, a host of friends and admirers came to revel in the joyous Purim feast with him.

Naturally, there was no lack of intoxicating spirits. In honor of Purim, drinks were plentiful—fine wine in big silver goblets and many confections. And, of course, Kozilek was present too, for he had to continually attend to the guests. When they went home after midnight, Reb Aharon and his family, thoroughly exhausted, fell into a deep slumber and slept sweetly.

But Kozilek used this event for his own purposes. He stole into the inner rooms of Reb Aharon's house and gathered up ten big silver goblets and about a dozen silver spoons and forks. He also took Reb Aharon Gins's silver watch and ran away that same night. No one saw him stealing and no one knew where he had fled.

When the theft was discovered the next morning, cries rang out in Reb Aharon Gins's house. And when they saw that Kozilek had disappeared, they realized at once that the robbery was his handiwork.

Reb Aharon sent for the two brothers and told them what their younger brother had done. "And I suspect that you lured him to do the stealing and that both the stolen goods and the thief are hidden at your house."

The two brothers began to argue with their boss about his suspicion. "We don't know a thing about it," they shouted, "and we can't possibly know where our brother has run off to, for he's an orphan with no family."

The two brothers did not want to reveal that they still had an elderly mother because they knew their brother had sought refuge with her. As soon as Reb Aharon would learn about their old mother he would surely rush there at once with policemen to search her house.

Reb Aharon informed the police chief about the theft and the latter sent his men to search the brothers' houses. But they found nothing suspicious in them. This whole incident deepened the brothers' hatred of Reb Aharon. Although they continued to work in his tannery, and had drawn their livelihood from it for ten years, they decided to take their revenge on him.

Late on Friday afternoon, just as the doors of the tannery were closing for two days, the two brothers made their way to their impoverished mother to find out what was happening there. Upon their arrival they saw their brother Kozilek lying in a sickbed. He could no longer speak for he was dying. After fleeing from Prague during the night, he had become over-heated while running and caught cold. At his mother's house blood spurted from his throat and, his body succumbing to the tuberculosis, he fell unconscious. He was still in bed when the brothers arrived on Friday night and died soon thereafter that same night.

The two brothers tried to have Kozilek buried on Sunday in the village cemetery. But since they had no money to pay the local priest for a proper Christian burial with all the traditional religious rituals, they took with them Reb Aharon Gins's watch that Kozilek had stolen.

They came to the priest with the following request: "Our mother's third son just died. She's a poor old widow without a penny to her name except for this silver watch she has from her husband. We brothers are poor too and the little bit of money we had we used for other burial expenses. That's why we're asking you to please take this silver watch in exchange for burial. We don't want to trouble you," they added, "to bury him with elaborate Christian ceremony. We just want permission to have him buried and we'll do that quietly."

The priest agreed. He took the watch from them and gave

them permission to bury their brother in the village's Christian graveyard. In the death registry book he recorded the day and date when Jan, son of Jadvina, was buried.

On Sunday evening, Kozilek was buried without fanfare by his mother, his two brothers, and the old gravedigger. Except for them no one knew of this, for Jadvina lived at the edge of the village near the cemetery. When they returned after the burial the two brothers sold all the stolen items in the village and gave their mother the money. Then they left her and returned to Prague.

The following morning, on Monday, the two brothers, exhausted from their journey, did not get to the tannery until noon. "Why so late?" an angry Reb Aharon rebuked them. "Why couldn't you come to work on time this morning?" Along with his reprimand he also heaped scorn on them about the theft. "And you no doubt got yourselves drunk these last two days and three nights with the money you got from the stolen goods."

This insult infuriated the two brothers. They were so enraged they could not even respond and proceeded to their work. But because they had their fill of their boss, they secretly decided that the time for revenge had come.

At night the two brothers conspired and pondered the

manner of vengeance against their master. They agreed on the following plan: Since no one knew where their brother Kozilek had fled to and no one in the village knew about their brother's death and burial, they could easily use this incident to initiate a blood libel against their boss by means of Kozilek's corpse.

That very week they chose a night to execute their evil scheme. The two brothers came to the village where Kozilek was buried. Under the cover of darkness, they opened his grave, stole his body from the coffin, and replaced the empty coffin in the grave so that no trace of their deed was noticeable. And as is their custom, they also put the symbol of their religion on the grave.

Then they slit the throat of the corpse with a knife to make it seem he had been slaughtered. They stripped Kozilek's body of the clothing and boots he usually wore in the house of his master, Reb Aharon, and wrapped him in a bloodstained white sheet. That night they journeyed to Prague with him and stopped by the Jewish cemetery, at the side where the road led from Prague to the next village, since that road was used by many travelers between those two points.

They dug a grave next to the cemetery fence and waited for a passing wagon with Christian riders, whereupon they began to lower the corpse into the ground. While so doing they spoke loudly, mockingly, and in an unruly manner in Yiddish, for they were fluent in that tongue. They did all this to attract the attention of passersby and to elicit questions about what they were doing here.

Just then a wagon with Christian passengers came by. When they heard the mocking tone of the gravediggers, they stopped the wagon.

"Who are you?" they asked, "and what are you doing here?"

"We're Jewish gravediggers," the two brothers replied in Yiddish, and then added, laughing: "When a wild, nasty, and filthy young fellow who was neither Jewish nor Christian died, the Jews didn't want to bury him in the cemetery but only under the fence. And since for us Jews it's a shame to bury such an abominable creature during the day, they told us to bury this corpse in the dark of night."

The Christian travelers accepted this explanation. Once they saw the body placed into the grave, they immediately resumed their journey to the next village.

The two brothers then took the bundle of clothes, the boots, and Kozilek's hat—all items very well known to all the tannery workers—put them into a bag, and set out for Prague. Then, under the cover of night, they sneaked into the cellar of Reb Aharon Gins's house and hid the bundle of Kozilek's clothes in a pile of sand they found there. They left while it was still dark and no one knew a thing about their evil deed.

The next morning the two brothers spread a rumor in several places where crowds gathered: "Some Christians who live in the village near Prague told us that two nights ago they saw Jews burying a gentile boy under the fence of the Jewish cemetery. These Jews said they were burying an atonement sacrifice." And to this rumor the two brothers added: "This must be the sacrifice of a Christian who has fallen into the hands of the Jews so they can mix Christian blood into their matzas, for it's a custom to call such a sacrifice an atonement."

This rumor flew quickly from one end of the city to the other. And, naturally, at that time there were many Jew-haters in Prague who for some years had been yearning to accuse the Jews of ritual murder but were unsuccessful. Now that they heard the story, with the passing of each day they began to spread it with increasing frequency. Some people began to inquire in all the Christian houses to learn if any Christian had disappeared recently.

The two brothers also helped to spread the nefarious rumor in the city. They let it be known quietly that they had learned from a trustworthy source that the sacrifice buried by the Jews was a Christian boy named Kozilek, who had worked for several years for the Jewish tannery owner, Reb Aharon Gins. When this Kozilek was hurt at the tannery, his master concluded that he was now very weak and no longer fit for work. Since the owner could not get rid of him, he hit upon the idea of using him as a sacrifice for the Passover holiday. On the night of their Purim feast, when the master had many guests and had drunk lots of wine, they also gave young Kozilek lots of wine to drink and made him so drunk he fell asleep. Then they brought him down to the cellar where they slaughtered him. To avoid falling under suspicion, the morning after the Purim feast the factory owner spread a rumor that Kozilek had robbed him the night before and fled.

What the brothers said spread with increasing intensity all over Prague until it reached the chief of police and his men. And inasmuch as many questions were being asked of him in high places as to why he did not thoroughly investigate this matter, he was obliged to intervene.

The police chief and his men went to that village near Prague. They rigorously questioned the Christians who had traveled that night and witnessed the burial. The latter described all they had seen. On his way back to Prague, the police chief brought along several villagers to point out where the burial had taken place. After the chief came home he sent a messenger to summon, one by one, the Maharal and the three heads of the community, each of whom was known as "the primus," as well as the two gravediggers.

He thoroughly questioned each of them separately and asked them to explain who was ordered to be buried beneath the cemetery fence. But each man gave the same reply: they knew nothing of this. They assured him that such an incident had never happened and that the anti-Semites were just looking for a pretext for a blood libel.

Then the police chief, accompanied by his officers and several Jewish gravediggers, went to the burial site where they looked for and found the grave. They took the corpse out of the grave, removed the dirty, bloodstained sheet, and lay the body on the ground in the presence of all the assembled in order to identify him.

Meanwhile a great crowd had gathered in front of the cemetery, among them the two brothers, who had secretly fabricated this entire misfortune. When the corpse was shown to the public, the two brothers burst out of the crowd and fell with their faces to the ground in front of the body.

"Ah, woe, my brother," they cried loudly, wailing and lamenting. First, they turned to the crowd and shouted, "Look!

Look what those damned Jews have done to us! Come and look, all of you, how the cursed Jew Aharon, that tannery owner, slaughtered our younger brother." Then they asked their friends and co-workers at the tannery to confirm that the dead boy was indeed the worker Kozilek. They recognized him at once.

The brothers pointed out the starkest sign for everyone to see—the missing two fingers of his right hand that doctors had amputated. The screams and wails of the two brothers agitated the mob. They became enraged and wanted to attack the Jews then and there and tear them to pieces. But despite the police chief's order to all the policemen and soldiers present to prevent violence, the crowd began throwing stones from afar at every Jew they saw.

A calamity was about to take place—an outbreak of violence against all Jewish homes. But the mob was thwarted only because of the Maharal's efforts. He rushed to the police chief and requested severe measures to ensure that no harm befall Jewish homes and property until the matter was brought before judges to determine beyond doubt whether the two brothers' claim was true or not.

"In the end, the truth will be revealed and everyone will see that this accusation is false," the Maharal assured him.

The police chief agreed with him and protected the Jewish Quarter from looting and violence.

But this did not stop the two Kozlovski brothers. "Make a thorough search of Reb Aharon Gins's cellar," was their further request of the police chief. "Rumor has it that our brother Kozilek was slaughtered in that very cellar. So you might very well find traces of his blood or other evidence to confirm the truth of the rumor."

The police chief was obliged to follow their suggestion. Along with many policemen and soldiers, as well as the two brothers and some of their friends who worked at the tannery, the police chief suddenly set upon Reb Aharon Gins's house. They made a thorough search, even digging into the earthen floor of the cellar and the pile of sand. There they found Kozilek's bundle of clothes, which the two brothers and their co-worker friends recognized at once.

Afterward, Reb Aharon Gins and his three sons-in-law were arrested; their wives and children were also brought to the jail. The police chief locked Reb Aharon Gins's residence and his tannery and placed the royal seal on them.

The following day many priests arrived carrying their flags, accompanied by a mass of people. They dressed the body of the boy in his clothes found in the cellar. Then they eulogized him amid sermons full of abuse and contempt against the Jews and bore him aloft with great honor to the cloister. Before taking him out for burial, the priests sent a message to the police chief with a request to bring the murderous Jew to the cloister. For according to the laws of their religion, the murderer had to confess his crime in the presence of his victim and beg his forgiveness.

The police chief could not contravene Christian law and, under heavy guard of many police and soldiers, had Reb Aharon Gins sent in chains to the cloister. When they placed him in front of the boy's body in the cloister, Reb Aharon was terrified. His face turned white as chalk. Then the head priest approached.

"Your hands have spilled this innocent blood and slit the throat of this corpse," he declared. "But you can now rectify your crime somewhat by asking the corpse for forgiveness and sewing up the dead boy's throat with your own hands."

"As my hands did not slit this throat," Reb Aharon replied, "so they will not sew up this throat."

The entire throng assembled there raged against Reb Aharon Gins. The crowd wanted to attack him and tear him apart like a fish for his impudence toward the priest. But the policemen and soldiers who surrounded Reb Aharon did not let anyone approach him.

The head priest then turned to Reb Aharon once more: "Can't you see how your crime has been revealed like the light of day?" he said. "The judges will no doubt sentence you to death. Therefore, I want you to know that if you confess before the corpse and sew up the throat you have slit, you will be doing your soul a favor and, if you'll only admit your guilt and tell us who enticed you to commit this crime, you won't come to heaven bearing such a burdensome sin."

"My soul doesn't need any favors," was Reb Aharon's reply, "for it is innocent of this crime."

Seeing they were getting nowhere with him, the priests ordered him returned to the prison. Then Kozilek was brought to the Christian cemetery in Prague with great pomp and splendor. Meanwhile, the Jews of Prague were terrified and filled with gloom. They feared walking the streets of the Christian quarter. And the city of Prague was dumbfounded.

This blood libel frightened the Maharal too and he went about sadly, for he also lost his credibility in the eyes of the authorities, who saw that all his hope was in vain. He had promised the police chief that soon the truth about this false accusation would surface, but now the opposite held true, since there was no defensible explanation for the bundle of Kozilek's clothing hidden in the sand in Reb Aharon Gins's cellar.

Although the Maharal knew full well that this was a false accusation and realized that this libel was cunningly engineered, he could not say anything and did not dare speak out now. And so he kept silent. Still, he ordered the entire community to publicly recite Psalms during all the morning services until the conclusion of the blood libel trial, not wanting to ordain a fast during the month of Nissan.

But this misfortune brought on another. The priests of Prague issued proclamations and warnings to the Christians to take care not to enter into Jewish homes, or even into their shops, for any Christian who entered a Jewish home could not be sure of his life and would be committing a deadly sin. The masses heeded the priests' warnings and the livelihood of the Jews came to an end.

Seeing the scope of this great calamity, which brought many other troubles in its wake, and sensing he had no more ideas how to bring about salvation, the Maharal directed a dream question to heaven. He got a clear answer composed of the following words: "You shall investigate and inquire and interrogate thoroughly" and "your children shall return to their land."

This answer invigorated the Maharal and caused him to rejoice. "Now there is hope the truth will be revealed," he consoled his congregation.

The day of the trial approached. On the first of Sivan, the day of the New Moon, the Maharal also sat in the courtroom. However, there were more irrefutable proofs to convict Reb Aharon than to exonerate him. In short, the judges rendered a guilty verdict against Reb Aharon Gins and his three sons-in-law and sentenced them to fifteen years of hard labor, while each of the wives was sentenced to six years' imprisonment. Only the children were exempt from punishment and were freed at once. This verdict saddened all the Jews of Prague, and the Maharal too was dejected.

Nevertheless, the Maharal, unable to sleep, did not rest nor was he still. It was absolutely clear to him that Kozilek had died suddenly from tuberculosis in the place to which he had fled, and there he was buried. Later, his brothers stole the body and brought it to Prague. They also stripped Kozilek's body of its clothing, stole into Aharon Gins's cellar, and hid them there. But it was difficult to prove this because, first of all, no one knew where Kozilek had run off to, and hence where he died; and second, how could this be confirmed if his real name, which had been recorded in the municipal records and in the death registry, was not known? For it was common knowledge that Kozilek was only a nickname and not his real name.

Therefore, the Maharal initiated an intensive inquiry to

learn where Kozilek could possibly have fled. And because logic would dictate that he ran to his place of birth, the Maharal tried to find out from Kozilek's co-workers at the tannery if they might have heard either from him or from the two Kozlovski brothers where they were born.

After much effort the Maharal succeeded in learning from the tannery workers that the brothers were born in a village four kilometers from Prague. The Maharal then sent wise and diligent men to that village to find out all they could about the Kozlovski family. There they discovered their family history and the address of their widowed mother. But they could not get the woman to say a word about her young son, Kozilek. "I haven't seen him since I sent him to his two bigger brothers," she insisted. "It seems to me he's in Prague working in the tannery with his two brothers."

The men returned to the Maharal with no further information. But when he heard that the mother's village was indeed the brothers' hometown and that it too had a Christian cemetery, the Maharal declared: "Now the way has been cleared for me to learn the truth and I will be obliged to use supernatural forces. Every dead man's soul," he added, "must hover over his grave no less than twelve months after his death, for during the first year the soul still has a slight connection with the body of the deceased. But if the dead person is not in his grave, then his soul is not discernible above the grave. However, not everyone, only men of lofty attributes—and animals, beasts, and birds too—can see these souls. And Yossele the golem has the capability to see these souls just like the animals, beasts, and birds."

That is why the Maharal asked the government to let him send two men to examine the outside of all graves dug during the last three months in that village's Christian cemetery. Thus he would be able to learn from which grave a body had recently been stolen.

To give him the authority to force the gravediggers to point out those graves to his emissaries, the Maharal asked the police chief: "Put your order in writing and send two policemen to me who will accompany my emissaries to examine the graves."

The police chief fulfilled the Maharal's request and sent two policemen along with his order to the village gravediggers bidding them to immediately show the two men all the new graves opened during the past three months.

The Maharal then summoned Yossele the golem to instruct him how to proceed and also sent with him a smart, capable man who too was told about their assignment. They undertook to carry out every one of the Maharal's commands.

The Maharal's two emissaries, accompanied by the two policemen, traveled to the village. After sending for the gravediggers, they all went to the Christian cemetery. The inspection commenced. Just as the Maharal, with his amazing insight, had expected, so it was, for Yossele the golem placed himself next to a grave and signaled it was empty; there was no corpse in it. One of the policemen rushed back to Prague and told this to the police chief. This news was also immediately conveyed to the Maharal.

The chief, accompanied by many of his men, went at once to the village; so did the Maharal and several community notables. The gravediggers opened the grave in their presence, removed the coffin, lifted the cover, and saw it was empty.

The police chief then immediately sent word to the village priest to bring him the church's birth and death registries. When the priest came, the chief demanded: "Tell me who was buried in this grave."

The priest looked and found that a few days after Purim a young boy named Jan, son of Jadvina, had been buried in this grave.

This information—that the mother of the Kozlovski brothers was named Jadvina—had already been known earlier to the first emissaries. The police chief then realized that Kozilek had indeed fled to his mother in this village and that he had died in her house and been buried in this grave. The two brothers then stole his body from the grave to initiate a blood libel in revenge against their master.

The police chief interrogated the priest meticulously to try to remember who had come to request a permit to bury the dead boy. "The two brothers of the dead youth came to me," the priest recalled, "but since they had no money to pay for a burial permit, they asked me to take a silver watch for the permit." The priest then took the watch from his pocket and showed it to the police chief.

When it was discovered that the silver watch was among the items stolen from Reb Aharon, the police chief took it and sent a quick carriage to the city. He asked the coachman to show the watch to Reb Aharon for him to confirm by any identifying marks whether it was his.

Even at a distance Reb Aharon immediately recognized his watch. Moreover, he mentioned an exterior mark and an also interior one, which was not visible from the outside. The coachman then sped back to the village and told the police chief that the prisoner had identified his watch at once. He showed the chief both the exterior and interior signs that Reb Aharon had mentioned.

The police chief's conclusion was that a false blood accusation had been secretly concocted against Reb Aharon. Accompanied by all his men, the chief now left the cemetery and burst into the widow's house.

"Where is your young son, Jan?" he bellowed.

"I haven't seen him since I sent him to his brothers in Prague to work in the tannery," Jadvina repeated her earlier denial, trying to conceal the matter even from the police chief.

But after the chief slapped her face twice, she fell to his feet, wailing and pleading, "Stop and I'll tell you the whole truth."

The policemen stood her up in front of the chief and she confessed, telling the entire story truthfully from beginning to end: "My young son came to me with the stolen items. He grew weaker and died in my house. Then his brothers came to visit him and buried him." She also told the chief where in the village the brothers had sold the stolen goods.

The police chief immediately ordered a search of that house, where they found all the stolen items.

"Who sold you all these things?" the chief demanded.

"The two Kozlovski brothers sold them to me," the buyer replied.

The chief ordered the arrest of both the widow Jadvina

and the man who had bought the stolen articles and sent them to the prison in Prague to stand judgment.

On his return to Prague, the police chief did not go home; rather, he and his entire force burst into the house of the two Kozlovski brothers to find and arrest them. But they were no longer at home, for they had surely heard that the truth would soon be known, prompting them to flee Prague to some unknown location.

The governmental authorities then concluded that the two brothers alone had secretly fabricated this blood libel. Reb Aharon Gins and all members of his family were immediately freed, and the city of Prague was festive and happy.

After this incident the Maharal's repute spread throughout the world and his fame in all the lands. Fear and dread overcame all the anti-Semites. In other countries too the furor over the blood libel abated. The Maharal then recorded this event from beginning to end in the form of a letter, as it is reported here, and sent it to King Rudolf. He also included a request for an audience with the king for he had something of great import to discuss with him face to face.

The king acceded to the Maharal's request. A few days later he sent a beautiful covered carriage with two high-ranking ministers to bring the Maharal to the king's palace. When the

Maharal appeared before the king he fell face down at his feet and wept. "Put an end," he implored, "to the evil anti-Semites who constantly aspire to pour scorn and humiliation on the Jews by means of the false accusation of ritual murder." The Maharal then asked the king: "Please issue an edict to all the courts in your land to annul all blood libel trials brought before them, for the sin of punishing and tormenting perfectly innocent people is borne by your entire kingdom."

The king was very astounded that the Maharal had fallen at his feet amid tears and pleading. He himself seized the rabbi's arm and requested of him: "Rise up from the floor."

The king honored the Maharal by offering him a seat next to him in a chair already prepared for him. The Maharal spoke to the king for an hour about certain matters and then was sent home with equally great honor—but he did not want to reveal what they had discussed. One week later the king promulgated an edict to all the courts in his domain prohibiting any further blood libel trials.

And the land was tranquil.

22

How the Maharal Brought
About the End of the Golem

AFTER THE PROMULGATION OF King Rudolf's new law abolishing blood libel trials in his domain, the Maharal noticed a period of calm. Another Passover holiday had come and gone, and nowhere in all the king's realm was there a hint of the blood libel misfortune. Then the Maharal summoned me, his son-in-law, Rabbi Yitzchok Katz, and his student and assistant in the rabbinic courtroom, Rabbi Yaakov Sasson Halevi, who with me had participated in the creation of the golem. "From this day on," the Maharal told us, "there is no longer any need for the golem, since blood libel trials are now prohibited in these lands."

This event took place on the night of Lag B'Omer, in 1590. The Maharal told Yossele the golem: "Tonight you will not sleep in the courtroom but rather carry your bed up to the attic of the Great Synagogue where you will lie down to sleep." The golem obeyed.

Now it was almost midnight, a time when no one sees or hears what is happening.

At two hours after midnight I, his son-in-law, Rabbi Yitzchok Katz, and his student, the rabbinic judge Rabbi Yaakov Sasson Halevi, stood before the Maharal. The rabbi, at his table, posed the following question to us: "Can a dead man like Yossele the golem transfer impurity to another person?"

The Maharal's incisive reasoning was that even if after his death the golem would remain flesh and bones like all other human beings, the issue of impurity was not applicable to him—especially since the Maharal had understood from the beginning that after the golem's death he would once again be a pile of clay and dust, just as he was before he was created.

Therefore, the Maharal took me up to the attic to participate in the death of the golem even though I am a kohen.

This is how the golem's life ended.

All three of us went up to the attic. The golem was asleep on his bed. The Maharal also permitted the old shamesh, Reb Avrohom Chaim, who held two lit tapers in his hands, to follow. But he was ordered to stand a bit further back.

All three of us stood by the golem's head. To bring about

his demise all we had to do now was reverse what we had done then when the golem had been formed and brought to life. And just as we had once stood at his feet facing his head and circled him seven times, starting on his right side, we now stood by his head facing his feet and began to circle him, starting on his left side, in order to withdraw from him his soul and spirit.

Now too we circled him seven times. Each circuit began on the left side of his head and continued around his feet to the right side of his head. Then we stopped and, following the Maharal's instructions, recited some combinations of letters. This we did after each of the seven circuits. The combinations of letters we recited now were the very same we had recited then during the creation of the golem, but now we said them backward.

Anyone who has an understanding of practical Kabbala and a thorough familiarity with the *Book of Creation* will grasp the secret of the creation process as well as the secret of annulling it.

After the seven circuits the golem remained lying on his bed like a lump of solid clay in the form of a man. Then the Maharal asked the old shamesh, Reb Avrohom Chaim, to approach. After the Maharal took the two tapers from his hands, we stripped the golem of all his clothes, except for his shirt. And since the attic contained many torn prayer shawls no longer fit for ritual use, Reb Avrohom Chaim gathered a few of them and we wrapped the golem's body with two old prayer shawls and tied them together.

Then we took the golem's rigid body and, obeying the Maharal's instructions, hid him under a big pile of tattered pages from damaged holy books that were stored in the attic so that no one would see where the golem was hidden.

"Bring the golem's bed and clothing down from the attic to the synagogue," the Maharal told the shamesh, "and to prevent anyone from noticing burn everything a little bit at a time."

Afterward, we all descended from the attic, washed our hands with water, and went to sleep. In the morning we spread the word that since something had angered the shamesh, Yossele the golem, he ran off during the night, but no one knew where. The masses in Prague believed this. Nevertheless, a mere handful of great men in the city who possessed lofty attributes knew the truth.

The second week after the golem's disappearance the Maharal proclaimed a ban: "No man or woman shall dare ascend to the synagogue attic and no longer may it be used as a storeroom for torn or damaged holy books."

His concern was obvious: people's carelessness with fire up there could easily cause a conflagration that would turn the entire synagogue into a roaring inferno. But the Maharal's close associates knew the real reason—not to make known where Yossele the golem lay hidden.

23

The Maharal's Remarks Concerning the Golem

MY SAINTLY TEACHER AND father-in-law, the Maharal, of blessed memory, said:

1. According to the law, the golem is not obliged to perform any of the mitzvas, even those incumbent upon a woman and a slave. But for the sake of appearances the Maharal ordered the golem to obey several mitzvas for everyone to see.

2. The golem did not even have the slightest hint of either the good or the evil impulse. Everything he did stemmed from his great dread that he would immediately cease to exist. All his actions were like those of an automaton.

3. Performing tasks up to ten cubits above and below ground posed no difficulty for the golem. Within those limits no barriers held for him.

4. The golem has the power to see spiritual things on a low level slightly higher than animals, beasts, and birds, and

slightly lower than demons and ghosts. Nevertheless, even a righteous man who possesses a divine soul and has free will cannot see spiritual things unless heaven grants him a special power for this purpose, as we read: "God opened her eyes."

5. The golem was created with a special power that prevents him from being killed with any weapon; neither can he be burned by fire nor drowned in water.

6. The Maharal was able to draw into the golem only a limited understanding, in keeping with his level of spirituality. But he could not imbue the golem with even a miniscule amount of wisdom and knowledge, since he was not worthy of having a divine soul either from internal or external radiance.

7. There was another reason the golem could not have been created with the power of speech: he was not worthy and suitable that the light of divine soul shine in him, for he only possessed the power of vital life and spirit, as it is written: "He breathed into his nostrils the breath of life and man became a living creature." The Aramaic translation states: "man became a speaking creature." Thus we see that the power of speech emanates only from the level of a divine soul.

8. Even though the golem does not possess a divine soul and hence cannot have the extra Sabbath soul, nevertheless, one could discern that on Sabbath his face was more lumi-

nous and appealing than on weekdays. And from this one can understand what the holy Zohar teaches: that on the holy Sabbath the dominion of demonic power is less intense than on weekdays. For these demons are in the category of darkness, while Sabbath holiness is in the category of immense light so powerful it crushes the dark forces. And the rays of light of Sabbath holiness spread throughout all the realms with such a great and mighty power that its influence even reaches to some small degree the great darkness which is the source of these demonic powers. And even though it is absolutely impossible to disseminate light directly to that place, it can still shine there as a reflected light. And thus the darkness is by itself diminished and the power of these demons is weakened—even in a great ignoramus who has no desire for this light and no concept of what is happening. In any case, some kind of spark of light from Sabbath holiness appears within him. And that is why our sages of blessed memory said that an ignoramus too is afraid of telling lies on the Sabbath.

9. The golem had to be created without the power of reproduction or desire for a woman, for if he had such desire—even if only on the level of beasts, which is much less than desire in human beings—he would have caused us enormous

trouble. Because of his great strength and vast power in this matter no woman would have been safe from him, as may be seen in the verse: "The sons of the gods saw how beautiful were the daughters of men and they took as wives any they liked."

10. That is why the golem was not subjected to any weakness or illness, for he had no desire that stemmed from the power of the evil impulse. Therefore, for him everything physical existed on a level proper and fitting for him, according to the criteria of his body, no more and no less. And if people like us could behave in like manner we would never experience weakness and disease.

11. That is why even without a clock the golem always knew the hour during a twenty-four-hour period, for during every hour of the day a different fine scent blows in mightily from the lower Garden of Eden and spreads immediately all over the world to cleanse the air we breathe and eliminate the poisons created in it. And the greatest danger is for human beings. For this the lower Garden of Eden had twenty-four kinds of fine scents that contain all the medications in the world. Moreover, many kinds of grasses and plants exist that absorb these fine scents, which is why they possess the power to cure several sorts of ailments.

When these twenty-four fine scents do not cleanse the air

properly or if this fine scent cannot reach a certain place, then an epidemic, God forbid, could break out. And because the golem's olfactory sense is at the proper level of perfection—since he never suffered from any kind of defect—each hour he is able to sense that hour's ascendancy of a different fine scent. And by virtue of this the golem can sense what hour it is. Minutes, however, he cannot discriminate. Every righteous person can achieve that level of sensitivity. And the most important thing is casting off one's physicality.

12. When the Maharal attempted to draw some life spirit into the golem, two spirits appeared before him, one of Yosef Sheyda, the other of Yonoson Sheyda. He chose the spirit of Yosef Sheyda, for he had already helped and saved Talmudic sages from many kinds of calamities, which was not the case with the spirit of Yonoson Sheyda. And, what is more, one can see from the Talmud that Yonoson Sheyda was not a master of mystical doctrine.

13. After his death the golem cannot transmit impurity to others because his body was not born, just made. Similarly, an animal created in like fashion does not have to be ritually slaughtered, nor does the prohibition of eating a limb torn from a living animal apply to it. If it is not considered a carcass it cannot transmit even a drop of impurity.

14. The golem's spirit will return at resurrection of the dead, but not in the first body of Yosef Sheyda, nor in the second body of Yossele the golem—but in a third body, formed by the union of a man and a woman. He will be drawn into this world before the coming of the Messiah by a righteous person, who will set aright something very necessary and of great import which is still an absolute secret—and he may be given the power to resurrect the golem's two previous bodies, as it is written: "He drew upon the spirit that was on him."

15. The golem will also have a share in the World to Come, not because he observed any particular mitzva of the 613 Commandments but because he saved Jews several times from great calamities. Even though he was obliged to do this, he is nevertheless worthy of reward, like a servant who is treated benevolently by his master—especially, since we see that when the golem was in the body of Yosef Sheyda he did not necessarily have to perform the good deeds he did but acted of his own free will.

16. All Jewish demons mentioned in the Zohar will be purified and have restitution by several transmigrations. Their spiritual repair will be accomplished not through Torah study or observance of mitzvas—for they were not present when the Torah was given at Sinai—but by doing good deeds for

Jews: saving them from misfortunes and persecutions, as did Yosef Sheyda. In this manner, they too will be worthy of the World to Come.

17. One does not have to study the combinations of letters as printed in the *Book of Creation* in order to create a man or an animal. A man who studies the combinations of letters only from this book will not be able to create anything. First, because of printers' errors and because much is missing. Second, and most important, is the comprehension in its own right that emanates from the person himself. He has to know at the outset which [spiritual] lights each letter hints at; then he will also understand of his own accord the physical powers inherent in each letter. This must be studied. And even after intensive study this matter is dependent upon the degree of the man's understanding and his righteousness, for if he is worthy he will attain this emanation and will understand how to combine the letters and create a creature in the physical world.

And even if this person writes these combinations of letters in a book, no one else will be able to make any use of them unless he knows how to meditate on the needed permutations by the power of his understanding. Otherwise, for him these combinations will merely be like a body without a soul. Bezalel had the greatest proficiency in this matter, for he could easily create a man or an animal. He also knew how to make permutations of letters that were used to create heaven and earth. Bezalel's knowledge, including all the 600,000 letters of our holy Torah, was achieved of his own accord through the power of his understanding. And even if he had written down the combination of letters in a book, no one else could have made any use of them if he lacked the ability of making the permutations on his own through the power of his understanding.

18. The second week after the death of the golem the Maharal prohibited anyone from going up to the synagogue attic under the pretext of fear of a fire breaking out in the huge pile of pages from old, torn, and tattered holy books stored there containing God's name. But he stipulated specifically that this prohibition is not applicable to any rabbinic judge who succeeded him in this rabbinic post in the holy community of Prague. He could ascend as long as he was not mortally afraid of a demon. The ban should not restrain him, but only on condition that he went up to the attic merely to look and not make any changes there.

19. Under no circumstances did the Maharal ever want to include the golem in a quorum of ten men. He said that even

according to the opinion that a woman can be included in a minyan the golem cannot be counted, since in this matter he is on a lower level than a woman, for in no way can he be considered an Israelite, as in the verse: "I will be sanctified in the midst of the Children of Israel." Women, however, are occasionally included in the category sons of Israel. Moreover, women in any case are obliged to abide by all the halakhic prohibitions of the Torah, which is not the case for the golem.*

Yitzchok ben Reb Shimson Katz, of blessed memory

*A Note by the Rabbi/Publisher

My friend, the great Torah scholar and pious man, who is a library unto himself, the honorable gaon, Rabbi David Hirsch, son of Rabbi Shlomo, long life to him, showed me Responsum 93 of the Chacham Tzvi wherein he expressed doubts that someone created by means of the *Book of Creation*—as we read in the Talmudic Tractate Sanhedrin, "Rava created a man"—can be included in a minyan. His grandfather, the gaon Rabbi Eliyahu, head of the rabbinic court in Chelm, also created a man, and he concluded that he cannot be included in a minyan.

24

A Miraculous Event Pertaining
to the Maharal's Engagement

THE GREATLY HONORED, WEALTHY, and renowned Reb
Shmelke Reich from the holy community of Worms took the
Maharal as a husband-to-be for his daughter, Perele, when he
was fifteen years old. He sent him to Przemysl to study in the
yeshiva of the gaon Maharshal, of blessed memory.

Meanwhile, however, the father-in-law, Reb Shmelke, had
become impoverished.

When the Maharal was eighteen, his father-in-law-to-be
wrote to him: "Because a young man of eighteen is a candidate for marriage, and because I am unable to offer you a
dowry, I don't want to bind you to honor your engagement
contract. Therefore, we herewith forgive you in advance and,
should you wish to break the engagement, give you permission to pursue another match as you see fit."

The Maharal wrote back to his future father-in-law: "I have no intention of going back on my word. Rather, I have hope in and anticipate the help of God. And so, if you do not want to bind your daughter, arrange a match for her first and then I will know I am free to make other arrangements."

But the father-in-law's fortunes did not improve and the engaged girl, seeing that her father was in a poor state, rented a little shop where she sold baked goods to help her parents earn a living. For ten years she sat there in solitude. The Maharal too did not wish to enter into another match and diligently studied Torah.

People called the Maharal "Reb Leib the Bachelor," and Rabbi Moshe Isserles, of blessed memory, said that of Reb Leib it is written: "I have exalted one chosen out of the people—I have found David my servant," for in him there is a spark of King David's soul, peace unto him.

This is how the match turned out.

During a war, hosts of troops came through the city. Following the soldiers was a knight. When he passed the bake shop of the Maharal's fiancée, with the tip of his spear he pierced a large loaf of bread that lay in the window. The engaged girl ran out to him in tears. "Don't steal the bread. I'm a poor maiden supporting my old and feeble parents."

"So what should I do if I'm starving for bread and don't

have any money to pay you?" the knight shouted at her. "But I can do this. Since I'm sitting on two pack-saddles, I'll give you one in exchange for the bread."

The knight pulled out one pack-saddle from under him and flung it with all his might into the shop. As the girl approached to pick it up, she was terror-stricken at seeing it was ripped open on one side and gold coins had fallen out of it. She struggled to lift the heavy pack-saddle full of gold dinars, then ran to tell her parents the news.

The father-in-law immediately wrote to the Maharal, inviting him to the wedding, for the Holy One Blessed Be He had helped him in a miraculous way to pay the dowry and arrange an honorable wedding as befits him.

I heard this story from my father-in-law, the Maharal of blessed memory, when he sat in judgment on a case pertaining to the abrogation of a match on account of poverty, where the in-law was unable to pay the promised dowry.

My father-in-law of blessed memory never wanted to participate in such a case; on the contrary, he tried his best to strengthen the bonds of a match. And only if the case demanded it did he send the litigants to the judges to adjudicate the matter in their home and not in his courtroom.

NOTES

Notice

page

3: *Notice* a kind of copyright notice.
    All who comply will prosper This and similar formulas are used
    in rabbinic writings as part of the copyright notice, telling read-
    ers they will be blessed if they obey the injunction.

1. *Publisher's Preface*

5: *Maharal* Acronym for **M**orenu **Ha-Ra**v **L**oeb (our teacher,
    Rabbi Loeb).
    gaon Genius; honorific title given to a learned rabbi.
    Yechezkel Landau Chief Rabbi of Prague (1713–1793), one of
    the great halakhic authorities of the eighteenth century.
    Known in Judah A classic compendium of 860 responsa (1776).
    Great Synagogue The Old-New Synagogue, or Altneushul, the
    nine-hundred-year-old synagogue that stands in the old Jewish
    Quarter of Prague.

6: *Yitzchok Katz* Katz is an acronym for **K**ohen **Tz**edek, or right-
    eous priest. In Chapter 8, Rosenberg calls him Yitzchok Cohen.

7:    *not be able to put it down* Literally, "devour it while it is still in his hand," based on Isaiah 28:4.

   The insignificant Ha-koton, in Hebrew; a designation of modesty traditionally appended to rabbinic writings.

2. *Bill of Sale*

8:    *Praised be God* The Hebrew has the two letters of *boruch ha-shem, B"H,* which can also mean "blessed be God" or "thank God." It usually appears at the top of letters or business documents written by traditional Jews.

   Yehuda Yudl Rosenberg The author's full name. Yudl is a short-hand form, or nickname, for Yehuda (Judah).

9:    *From this moment on . . . another copy of the above manuscript* Such wording is traditional in copyright notices in rabbinic writings.

   5669 The year according to the traditional Jewish calendar, equivalent to 1909.

3. *The History of the Great Gaon, the Holy, Supernal Maharal of Prague, May the Memory of that Righteous, Saintly Man Be a Blessing for Life in the World to Come*

10:    *Worms* Southern Germany. In Worms, 450 years earlier, the great commentator Rashi studied.

   5273 from the time of creation, according to the Jewish calendar; or 1513.

   the Christian nations . . . claimed the Jews needed Christian blood for their Passover matzas the centuries-old European Christian accusation against the Jews known as the blood libel.

12: *"This one will comfort us . . ."* Genesis 29:5.

Leib The Hebrew text says Liva, another form of Loeb or Leib, all meaning "lion."

"Judah is a lion's whelp . . ." Genesis 49:9. Judah is the English version of the Hebrew Yehuda, a name that among European Jews was always coupled with "Loeb," "Leib," or "Loew"— the Yiddish and German word for "lion."

4. The Maharal's Battle Against the Blood Libel

13: *"A man who excels at his work shall attend upon kings."* Proverbs 22:29.

King Rudolf He became Emperor of the Holy Roman Empire and King of Bohemia in 1576.

14: *stand straight as a wall* Based on the verse in Exodus 15:8, "The floods stood straight as a wall . . ." with its echoes of God saving the Israelites from the Egyptian attackers.

5. The Maharal's Suggestion to Have a Disputation with the Priests

16: *the Jews in Prague . . . fasted on Mondays and Thursdays* Fasting on Mondays and Thursdays, the weekdays on which the Torah is read at morning services, was a traditional practice of Jewish communities during times of trouble, as was the recitation of psalms from the Book of Psalms.

6. *The Disputation*

18: *defiles even by proximity* Literally, "defilement of tents"; figuratively, under one roof—or defilement by proximity. See Mishna Sabbath 2:3.

    Sadducees A sect composed mostly of the wealthier, more conservative Jews who believed only in the written Torah, not Oral Law.

19: *Pharisees* A sect that believed in both the written Torah and Oral Law that eventually evolved into mainstream Judaism.

    Essenes A religious, monastic sect, few in number, who lived by the Dead Sea, closer in outlook to the Pharisees than the Sadducees.

20: *"As a father has compassion of his sons."* Psalms 103:13.

    When the son pleaded with his father The author is probably referring to the famous passage in the New Testament, Mark 15:32, where Jesus quotes Psalms 22:2, saying, "My God, my God, why hast Thou forsaken me?"

21: *Adam's sin* The Hebrew words for the Christian concept of original sin.

    Isaac the son of Abraham wanted to be sacrificed This concept is not Biblical but appears in post-Biblical midrashic sources.

    relief and deliverance Esther 4:14.

22: *repaying evil for good* Proverbs 17:13.

    Joseph the Righteous In post-Biblical literature, Joseph is called such for having withstood the temptations of Potiphar's wife. Genesis 39:7–13.

    "Although you intended to harm me, God intended it for good . . . for the survival of many people" Genesis 50:20.

    the Jews who sentenced Jesus to death Probably referring to the

Sadducee priests who were despised by everyone, although the death sentence was not rendered by the Jews. Crucifixion was a typical Roman method of execution.

23: *Israel is my first-born son* Exodus 4:22.

Covenant of the Pieces Genesis 15:13, where God tells Abraham that his descendants will be enslaved and oppressed for four hundred years.

Pharaoh declared, "I do not know the Lord" Exodus 5:2.

25: *Even though he sinned he is still a Jew* Babylonian Talmud, Sanhedrin 44a.

27: *You have chosen us from among all other nations* The opening phrase of a prayer recited during the Silent Devotion of all three major festivals: Passover, Shavuot, and Sukkot. In the Babylonian Talmud, Yoma 87b, a fourth-century sage named Ula bar Rav states that this is a well-known prayer.

a minimal burden and easy work This parable is very likely based on the Midrash in Genesis Rabbah 2:2, where a king buys two servants; one would eat from the king's bounty, the other had to work hard to eat.

7. "A Man Who Excels at His Work Shall Attend upon Kings." This is the Maharal

31: *Shevat* Hebrew name of a month that falls in January/February.

happy and of good cheer Esther 5:9. There is some irony here, for the phrase in Esther is applied to Haman's joy at achieving his nefarious plan against the Jews.

32: *fear of . . . fell upon the[m]* Esther 8:17.

32: *he possesses the spark of* Possession of sparks is a kabbalistic concept.

Ishbi-benob II Samuel 21:16. The name of a Philistine adversary who tried to kill David. For Rosenberg the Philistines symbolize the enemy, while David, of course, is the symbol of Israel's continuity and the source of the Messianic line.

33: *mirror of cast metal* Job 37:18; "mirror" is also mentioned in Exodus 38:8.

8. *How the Maharal Created the Golem*

34: *asked a question during a dream* Seeking a solution to a problem by asking a question during a dream stems from the medieval period.

answer came from heaven In the Hebrew the ten-word sentence is in alphabetical order; it begins with *aleph,* continues with *bet,* and so on until the tenth letter, *yud.*

In the mystical tradition, the Hebrew alphabet has a special power. Indeed, the Agada speaks of a link between Creation and the letters of the Torah. Genesis Rabbah 12:2 states that God created the heavens and the earth with the letter "hey" [h], the second letter of the two-letter name of God, *yah.* And the *Book of Creation* (see note below) considers the letters of the alphabet and their combination as cosmic powers and asserts that the world was created by means of the Hebrew *aleph bet.*

The first ten primordial numbers and the twenty-two letters of the alphabet combine to form their own potency, known in Kabbala as "the thirty-two paths to wisdom." Therefore, the first ten letters of the alphabet, especially if they appear in a sentence that is in alphabetical order (as are some Psalms, some chapters in Proverbs and Lamentations, and a number of Hebrew prayers), intensifies its potency. The power of the number ten is also reflected in the Ten Commandments.

To imitate the alphabetical order of this ten-word line in English translation would be awkward and distortive, and also meaningless for the English reader.

34: *combinations of names* From Kabbala. Combinations of letters into words that form the Divine Name.

summoned me This is the first time the narration moves into the first person.

35: *four elements, fire, air, water and earth* In medieval physics, the four basic components of the universe.

walk around the golem seven times A magical number. The bride also walks around the groom seven times in a traditional wedding ceremony.

36: *". . . and the man became a living creature"* Genesis 2:7.

Book of Creation Sefer Yetzira, third–sixth century C.E., one of the oldest Hebrew mystical texts, accenting speculative thought and cosmogony; a seminal kabbalistic text.

gazed at us in wonder See Genesis 24:21.

shamesh Beadle, sexton, assistant. Plural: *shamoshim.*

37: *spirit of Yosef Sheyda* Babylonian Talmud, Pesachim 110a. Yosef Sheyda's name is very likely Rosenberg's source for the golem's name.

38: *an unfinished vessel* Mishna Kelim 12:6.

Yossele A Yiddish diminutive of Yosef, which in English is Joseph.

10. *How Yossele the Golem Caught Fish for Rosh Hashana*

42:    *Mincha time* The Afternoon Service, the last of the three obligatory daily services.

43:    *help them observe mitzvas* The "mitzva" of eating fish on Rosh Hashana—a folk custom widely observed in Europe, even though it wasn't really a mitzva (a commandment).

12. *The Maharal's First Miracle with the Golem*

49:    *pursuing him relentlessly* Based on Isaiah 14:6.

13. *The Astonishing Tale of the Healer's Daughter*

50:    *strayed from the straight and narrow path* Jeremiah 2:23.

52:    *coached her to tell* Based upon Jeremiah 9:4.

55:    *knew nothing of the events [in town]* Jonah 4:11; literally, "doesn't know his right hand from his left hand."
In the middle of the night Exodus 12:29 and other places. A well-known phrase from the Torah and the Passover Hagada.

56:    *in turmoil* Based on Job 41:23.
King Rudolf's edict See opening of Chapter 7, where Rudolf's edict is promulgated.
thoroughly investigate Mishna Sanhedrin 4:1.

58:    *request and plea* Esther 5:7.

59:    *recite the Book of Psalms* A traditional Jewish practice in times of trouble.
Great Synagogue The Altneushul.

60:    *The mute . . . nodded [and] put his finger in his mouth.* Rosenberg is making his own variation on the old "debate by signs" motif that runs through Western and Jewish folklore back to Greco-Roman times. See a marvelous example in Rabelais' *Gargantua and Pantagruel*, Book II, Chapter 18–19. In this tradition, the signs mean one thing to one person and another to the other man. In *Golem,* the mute's sign signifies drink for him but blood guilt to the anti-Semitic priest. I remembered reading one such debate in Jewish folklore but couldn't locate it. Enter Gilad Gevaryahu, who sent me the story "Jews Versus Pope." Here a simple Roman Jew, Moishe, debates the Pope, who has ordered the Jews to leave Rome in three days. When the Pope lifts three fingers (to signify the Trinity), Moishe raises one (one God). This is the Pope's interpretation. Moishe sees the three fingers as three days to leave town; he waves one finger to say not one of us will leave.

61: *smooth-tongued* Proverbs 26:28.
66: *"his head covered in mourning"* Esther 6:12.
the city . . . rang with joyous cries Esther 8:15.

14. *The Wondrous and Famous Story Known as "The Daughter's Misfortune"*

69: *to recall something he had forgotten* Based upon Mishna Ta'anit 2:4.
70: *wine of libation* Hence, not kosher, for it had been dedicated to Christian sacred purposes.
71: *feeling a change of heart* Based on Hosea 11:8.
73: *He consoled her* Isaiah 40:2.
74: *When the wine had made their hearts merry* II Samuel 13:28.
to present herself to a handsome intended groom Reminiscent

of Esther's presenting herself to King Ahasuerus. Esther, chapter 2.

74: *wine feast* Esther 7:8.

prepared another great feast Again like Esther's second banquet. Esther, chapter 7.

75: *all their labor was in vain* Based on Job 39:16. The Book of Job is read in a mourner's house. And just as quotes from Esther reflect joy, a line from Job indicates gloom.

neither rescuer nor deliverer The phrases "no rescuer" and "no deliverer" appear many times in the Bible; for instance, "no rescuer" in Hosea 13:4 and "no deliverer" in Hosea 5:14, but they never appear together in one Biblical verse.

76: *kinsman and rescuer* Ruth 2:20.

vengeful and vindictive Based on Leviticus 19:18.

77: *fast for three days* Esther 4:16.

78: *cast them behind her back* I Kings 14:9.

Unable to restrain herself Genesis 45:1, where the subject (Joseph) is masculine.

her distress Genesis 4:6. Literally, "her face had fallen."

83: *he was exceedingly agitated* Esther 4:4, where the subject (Esther) is feminine.

84: *the bitterness of death* I Samuel 15:32.

his compassion was stirred Jeremiah 31:19.

he had no peace of mind. Literally, "his bones knew no tranquility"; Job 20:20, but there the phrase has "belly" instead of "bones."

86: *Tosfos Yom Tov.* Yom Tov Lipmann Heller (1579–1654), rabbi and author of *Tosfos Yom Tov,* a supplementary commentary to Obadiah of Bertinoro's classic commentary to the Mishna.

the Hebrew first name Avrohom The name given to all male converts, to link them to the first Jew, Abraham.

Yeshurun Isaiah 44:2, a poetic name for the People of Israel.

89: *dismissed with flimsy excuses* Babylonian Talmud, Hullin 27b; literally, pushed him away with a straw.

91: *He could no longer contain himself* Like Joseph in Genesis 45:1.

for no harm will befall you Psalms 91:10.

92: *over the paths of the seas* Psalms 8:9.

Now we can see with certainty Isaiah 52:8.

enjoy your acquisition Babylonian Talmud, Ketubot 10b.

93: *kashered* Referring to affixing mezuzot on the doorposts, boiling the silverware to make it kosher, and other steps to make the kitchen kosher.

wonders and miracles A phrase from the Siddur.

94: *bes medresh* A small synagogue; a place to study.

Kloyz Another word for prayer house.

15. A Very Amazing Tale About a Blood Libel by the Priest Thaddeus Which Caused His Final Downfall and His Banishment from Prague

96: *search for leaven* On the night before the first Seder, Jews conduct a ceremonial search for leaven by leaving bread crumbs on the window sills of most rooms and then, with the children, they "search" for it with a candle, feather, and wooden spoon. This leaven, or *chametz*, is burned the following morning.

All the leaven An Aramaic passage stating that all leaven in the household has been eliminated.

Siddur Prayer book.

97: *colors that signify lovingkindness . . . judgment . . . compassion* A kabbalistic concept.

97:   *Avoda* A portion of the Yom Kippur Musaf Service where the can-
      tor narrates the High Priest's Yom Kippur ritual in the Temple.
      crimson thread Babylonian Talmud, Yoma 67a. "At first they [the
      kohanim; i.e., the priests] would tie a crimson thread (or strap)
      to the doorway of the hall [the entrance hallway to the Holy
      Temple]. If it turned white they [the people] were happy [for
      their sins were forgiven]; if not, they felt sad and shameful."
          Also, during the *Avoda,* the High Priest's Yom Kippur ser-
      vice, a crimson thread was bound on the head of the goat that
      was dispatched over a cliff.
      turned white In Isaiah 1:18, we read: "Though your sins be as
      scarlet they will become as white as snow." This is no doubt
      the ultimate source for all the color change passages in Rosen-
      berg's *Golem.*
      the crimson letters did not turn white Moshe Idel, the noted
      Hebrew University authority on Kabbala, notes in *Golem,* his
      study of the golem throughout history, that kabbalists, during a
      moment of ecstatic experience, would see colors enwrap the
      divine names. Further, he writes that letters were visualized in
      various colors. Rosenberg may have been aware of this tradition
      and adapted it for this scene, having the Maharal declare that
      whereas the words usually turn white, to signify purity, this
      year they did not.
          When I asked Daniel Matt, the contemporary translator of
      the Zohar, where in Moses Cordovero's *Pardes Rimmonim* I
      could find a citation about letters changing colors, he wrote
      that he "wasn't able to find anything on colors changing, just a
      reference to the four letters of the Tetragrammaton, each with
      its own color." Matt adds that in another kabbalistic text there
      is a reference to letters of the alphabet that change to several

gavnin, "a word that usually refers to color but in context can also mean 'kinds.'"

On the other hand, this passage may very well be Rosenberg's invention—as are so many other aspects of his imaginative book—and if indeed his own creation, a particularly striking one.

98: *in my possession* The next words in the formula.

Jacob I.e., the people of Israel; the Jews.

the Light of Israel Referring to great men. In the Bible, a leader, David, II Samuel 21:17; in the Talmud, a scholar, Yochanan ben Zakkai, Berakhot 28b. In this chapter it refers both to Jews and the Maharal.

the Great Sabbath The Sabbath before Passover.

99: *his son-in-law, the gaon, our saintly master, Rabbi Yitschok Katz* Rosenberg slips up here for, if as he avers, Katz is the narrator of the book, he would have used the first person singular and said simply, "me," as he did in Chapter 8, p. 34.

100: *trap and snare* Joshua 23:13.

a fire has come out of Numbers 21:28.

101: *bitter enemy of the Jews* Like Haman, Esther 3:10.

pit he had dug Proverbs 26:27.

106: *"The Guardian of Israel neither slumbers nor sleeps"* Psalms 121:4.

girded his strength Jeremiah 1:17.

I will rely on The author here uses an image from the Penitential Prayers for Yom Kippur.

No harm befalls those who are sent on a pious mission Babylonian Talmud, Pesachim 8a.

where danger is to be expected Pesachim 8b.

107: *You who dwell in the shelter of the Most High* Psalms 91:1. The thought continues in verse 2, "my refuge, stronghold, my God in whom I trust." Traditionally recited at times of fear.

109: *as empty-handed as they had come* Based upon Exodus 21:3.

the trap has been broken and we have fled to safety Psalms 124:7.

Rock of Israel and its Redeemer This phrase, a popular designation for God, drawn from Isaiah 44:6, "King of Israel and its Redeemer," and Isaiah 30:29, "Rock of Israel," is used at certain times in the Ashkenazic tradition in the festival Evening Service just before the Silent Devotion.

110: *not a trifling matter* Deuteronomy 32:47.

111: *grew sick of living* Genesis 27:46.

an uninhabited land Leviticus 16:22.

so may all the wicked enemies of Israel perish Based on Judges 5:31.

protecting the esteemed woman A hymn by Yishai ben Mordechai that begins, "A pious man once there was . . ."

112: *Shekhina* A feminine noun in Hebrew, the only name of God that is grammatically feminine.

Five, said the woman to him Rosenberg is bending the text in order to come up with that sentence. In the hymn one sentence ends with the word "five" (". . . and also children five"), while the next line begins with "Said the woman . . ." By ignoring punctuation Rosenberg can have the Maharal use midrashic license and say, "Five, said the woman."

16. The Marvelous Story of the Wonder of Wonders that the Maharal Revealed to the Two Berls Whose Two Children Were Switched by a Midwife

113: *children's teacher* Babylonian Talmud, Bava Batra 21b.

114: *In the matter of children* The author uses the opening words of the weekly portion from Genesis 25:19 that lists offspring: "These are the generations of . . ."

she was overcome with compassion I Kings 3:26. There the subject too is a baby.

115: *taken away my disgrace* Based on Genesis 30:23, where Rachel gives birth to her first son, Joseph.

went to the ritual bath the same night Since women usually go to the ritual bath somewhere near the middle of their cycle, it is a time conducive to conception.

116: *cries of approval* based on Zechariah 4:7.

117: *The boys grew up* Genesis 25:27.

120: *the Maharal handed him* [the golem] *his staff* This scene—the rabbi sends an aide to the cemetery with his staff to call a dead soul to a trial; the synagogue trial behind a screen; the dead soul's testimony; the men's terror—is so like the trial in Anski's play, *The Dybbuk* (1918), I'm sure he was influenced by *The Golem.*

122: *down to the last detail* Deuteronomy 27:8; literally, "explain it well."

123: *"my soul will be bound up in the bond of everlasting life"* A phrase traditionally recited, in the third person, for one who is dead; this phrase is also inscribed on a tombstone, using the initial letters of each word.

17. The Astounding Story of the Torah That Fell to the Floor on Yom Kippur

127: *lifting up the Torah* When the Torah reading is completed, two men are called up to the bimah, one to lift the Torah high; the other to bind the scroll and cover it with its mantle.

Eve of Sukkos The fall harvest festival, occurring in September-

October. If the holiday begins, let us say, Monday at sundown, all day Monday is considered the Eve of Sukkos. Hence, the fast would take place one day earlier, on Sunday. It was customary for the congregation to fast when a Torah fell.

127: *the Rock of Israel does not desire fasts* Despite its Biblical resonance, these words are not from the Bible but are loosely based upon Isaiah 59:5 and 6.

128: *felt sad of heart* Literally, "his face fell," Genesis 4:6.
defile yourself with her Leviticus 18:20. The Torah reading for Yom Kippur has a list of forbidden relationships, including the passage cited here.

18. The Attack on Yossele the Golem

130: *bastard* Not just a curse word but in Hebrew signifying the child of an adulterous union.
Spain and Italy 1492. By Italy, the author means Sicily. Later, Jews were expelled from southern Italy.

132: *a few smacks* Literally, "a gift of the hand," Deuteronomy 16:17.

133: *bruise for bruise* Exodus 21:25.
Let's deal shrewdly with Based upon Exodus 1:10.
water . . . heated up for his enjoyment Babylonian Talmud, Sabbath 119b: "Hot water at the end of Sabbath is a pleasure."

134: *Havdala* The prayer recited on Saturday night marking the end of the Sabbath.

135: *barely alive* Based on Job 27:3.

19. An Awesome Tale About the Ruin Near Prague

139: *playing on a big flute* One would have expected the author to use "bugle" or "trumpet," for which a Biblical Hebrew word exists.

the demonic pest A phrase from the Morning Service. Depending on context can be variously rendered as "demon" or "nuisance."

140: *His flesh grew lean* Psalms 109:24.

weak with hunger Based on Psalms 107:5.

ritual fringes Numbers 15:37–41, the command for the four-cornered garment with fringes.

141: *hand tefillin was also found to have a flaw* Common belief that if a man has problems, the ritual fringes and/or the tefillin probably contain a defect.

"For he will order His angels to guard you wherever you go" Psalms 91:11.

gematria A method of interpreting Biblical verses by figuring the numeric value of a word's letters, then finding another verse or word of equal value and showing they are related.

kosher parchment On sheepskin, or from any other kosher animal.

No dog shall bark at any of the Israelites Exodus 11:9.

20. *A Wondrous Tale About Duke Bartholomew*

143: *one could meditate* Genesis 24:63.

145: *When wine goes in, secrets go out* A Hebrew proverb.

who was alive and who had died Variation on II Samuel 15:21.

147: *he feared the boy might convert* The duke is assuming (for surely the author, a rabbi, would know better) that since the youngster was being raised in a Christian home, if he found out he was Jewish, he would seek to return to Judaism. In actuality, since the boy is Jewish by birth, despite the Christian influences around him, there would be no need for him to convert.

151:    *wise and intelligent* Based upon Job 34:35.

        True World Another name for heaven.

154:    *He turned this way and that but saw no one* Exodus 2:12.

155:    *Beis Yaakov* House of Yaakov, or Jacob.

        on the contrary Esther 9:1, echoing the similarity in the Esther story, where tragedy turns into salvation and celebration.

        with a cheerful countenance Ethics of the Fathers 1:15: "Greet everyone with a cheerful countenance."

        for they obviously could not be buried in the Jewish cemetery either A puzzling remark, for they were both Jewish and could indeed have been buried in a Jewish cemetery. Very likely the author added this detail for the dramatic aspects of lonely burial.

21. *The Last Blood Libel in Prague During the Maharal's Lifetime*

156:    *learned and prosperous* Babylonian Talmud, Menahot 53a.

        Torah learning and eminence were combined Babylonian Talmud, Berakhot 53b; literally, attained two tables.

157:    *"Kozilek"* In Polish, a young billy goat.

159:    *hard labor* Midrash Exodus Rabbah 5, and based upon Exodus 1:13.

        He was disgusted with his life Based upon Genesis 27:46.

160:    *drinks were plentiful* Esther 1:8.

161:    *made their way* Psalms 85:14.

162:    *sickbed* Psalms 41:4.

163:    *so late* Based on II Samuel 20:5.

        they had their fill Babylonian Talmud, Sotah 9a.

172:    *And the city of Prague was dumbfounded* Esther 3:15. "And the city of Shushan was dumbfounded."

his hope was in vain Job 11:20.

defensible explanation Mishna Sandhedrin 4:1.

173: *month of Nissan* Usually April, when Passover falls and no fasts are permitted during that month.

committing a deadly sin Ethics of the Fathers 3:5.

no more ideas Psalms 13:2.

"You shall investigate and inquire and interrogate thoroughly"; "your children shall return to their land" A line composed of two Biblical verses, Deuteronomy 13:15 and Jeremiah 31:17.

174: *irrefutable proofs* A phrase first used by Maimonides in his Letter to the Sages of Castille.

175: *she insisted* Based on Job 23:13.

no further information Psalms 19:4; literally, "no utterance and no words."

180: *the city of Prague was festive and happy* Esther 8:15. Just as previously the city was dumbfounded at the bad news, now, as in the Esther story, the city rejoices at good news.

181: *And the land was tranquil* Judges 3:11. A phrase marking a period of tranquility in the Land of Israel.

22. How the Maharal Brought About the End of the Golem

182: *Lag B'Omer* A traditional day of celebration.

183: *transfer impurity to another person* Since he is not a fully created human being, he is not capable of doing this. See Chapter 23.

kohen A kohen, a member of the priestly class, cannot be near the dead or participate in funerals, except for those of close family members.

184: *And just as we had once stood at his feet facing his head and circled him seven times . . . we now stood by his head facing his feet* Rosenberg must have been familiar with the anonymously written thirteenth-century Commentary on Sefer Yetzira that states that in creating a golem one moves forward while reciting the letters, but if one wants to destroy that creation he goes backward. But nothing in that book suggests a backward recitation of the letters. However, Rosenberg may have seen the kabbalistic text *Or ha-Hamah,* published in Poland in 1886, which mentions the recitation of letters backwards to undo creation. Two other medieval kabbalists suggested the same procedure: R. Azriel of Gerona in his *Commentary on Sefer Yetzira* and R. Joseph Ashkenazi in a work with the same title.

184: *Book of Creation Sefer Yetzira.* Of course, no formula for golem-making can be found in this book. However, most kabbalistic writings that mention creating a golem refer to this influential book.

185: *wrapped the golem's body with two old prayer shawls* It is customary to bury a Jewish man with his tallit, one of whose fringes has been removed, signifying it is no longer usable.
tattered pages from damaged holy books Torn pages of holy texts containing God's name that are no longer used are either stored or buried. They may not be discarded.
washed our hands with water As is traditional after a funeral.

23. *The Maharal's Remarks Concerning the Golem*

188: *"God opened her eyes"* Genesis 21:19, referring to Hagar.
neither can he be burned by fire nor drowned in water Compare Isaiah 43:2.

"He breathed into his nostrils the breath of life and man became a living creature." Genesis 2:7. He, i.e., God.

Aramaic translation Of Onkelos, a second-century C.E. translator of the Five Books of Moses into Aramaic, included in almost all printed Hebrew Bibles.

190: *"The sons of the gods . . ."* Genesis 6:2.

for during every hour of the day a different fine scent blows in I have been unable to find any source for this, which may also be one of Rosenberg's inspired inventions. The closest text to something changing "every hour" is a passage in the anonymous *Sefer Ha-Hayyim* (c. 1200), which mentions the creation of an artificial man. Quoted in Moshe Idel's *Golem,* the passage begins: "The thoughts of men change every hour . . ." In the back of Rosenberg's *Sefer Refoel Ha-Mal'akh* (The Book of the Angel Refoel) a small book of folk remedies, is a table that lists the combination of letters that are efficacious every hour. This kabbalistic material also no doubt inspired Rosenberg to create this imaginative passage.

192: *Yosef Sheyda* Babylonian Talmud, Pesachim 110a. A demon who tells the sages about the customs of demons. The word "sheyda" contains the Hebrew word for demon, "sheyd."

"He drew upon the spirit that was on him." Numbers 11:25, referring to Moses.

194: *Bezalel* Exodus 36:1. God gives Bezalel the understanding to construct the Tabernacle and its equipment.

195: *the Children of Israel* Leviticus 22:32. "Bnai yisroel" translates literally as "sons" of Israel but means Children of Israel, People of Israel, Israelites, or Jews.

halakhic prohibitions Commandments that begin with "Do

not . . ." (i.e., "Do not work on Sabbath . . ."). Also known as negative commandments.

195: *Responsum 93 of the Chacham Tzvi* Published in Amsterdam, 1712. A responsum is a halakhic response to a question written to a rabbi, asking him for a decision on a Jewish legal matter.

24. *A Miraculous Event Pertaining to the Maharal's Engagement*

196: *Maharshal* Acronym of **M**orenu **Ha-R**av **Sh**elomo Luria (1510–1574), a Polish Talmudic scholar.

a young man of eighteen is a candidate for marriage Ethics of the Fathers 5:24.

we herewith forgive you in advance An engagement was considered even stricter than a marriage and breaking an engagement was considered a serious offense, involving request of forgiveness.

197: *Moshe Isserles* The eminent Polish halakhic authority and codifier (1525–1572).

"I have exalted one chosen . . ." Psalms 89:20, 21. In Hebrew, the word for "bachelor," *bokher,* or "young man," also means "one chosen."

About the Author: The most famous and influential of Yudl Rosenberg's twenty-seven books, almost all of them in Hebrew, was *The Golem*. Born in Poland in 1859, and a rabbi by profession, he wrote on Jewish law, translated parts of the kabbalistic text, The Zohar, into Hebrew, and wrote other works of fiction. He died in Canada in 1935.

About the Editor/Translator: Curt Leviant is the prize-winning author or translator of more than twenty books. Among his six critically acclaimed novels are *The Yemenite Girl, Diary of an Adulterous Woman,* and *Ladies and Gentlemen, the Original Music of the Hebrew Alphabet and Weekend in Mustara* (two novellas). His many translations from Yiddish include works by Sholom Aleichem, Chaim Grade, and Isaac Bashevis Singer. Mr. Leviant has won the Wallant Award for his fiction and several national and international literary fellowships, including those of the National Endowment for the Humanities and the National Endowment for the Arts.